"CAREFUL, BABY!"

He warned in voice gone calm with controlled anger.

"Careful, my eye! Just because you think I'm still eight years old doesn't mean other men do, Russell! I'm grown up! I wish I'd never..oh, you horrible, cold blooded!" She choked on the words, a sob tearing out of her throats as the tears rolled down her cheeks.

"You damned little fool," Russell said in a strange, tight voice. His hands cupped her face and he bent to put his mouth against her wet eyes, sipping the tears from her closed eyelids in a slow, smoldering intimacy that took her breath away. His teeth caught her full lower lip, nipping at it sensuosly.

"Open your mouth for me," he growled huskily, "show me how grown up you are, Tish."

"Russell..." she choked, her breath strangling her, the brushing, nibbling, coaxing pressure of his tormenting mouth making tremors all over her body. "The...storm...."

His mouth opened on hers, pressing her lips apart in a burning, hungry silence that winded her.

"It's in me," he murmured against her mouth, "and in you, hungry and sweet and wild. Don't talk. Kiss me...."

NOW AND FOREVER

Diana Palmer

A Macfadden Romance/New York

A MacFadden Romance

Kim Publishing Corp.
432 Park Avenue South
New York, N.Y. 10016

ISBN CODE 0-89772-144-6

CHAPTER ONE

The sky was a blaze of color above the foaming whitecaps, and only the free cry of gulls broke the watery whisper of the waves that teased the shore. Lutecia Peacock closed her eyes and sat like a slender statue. Her back cold against the strength of the boulder at the water's edge, she sat drinking in the peace and seclusion of sea and sand.

Farther down the beach, Frank Tyler was just coming out of the water, his pale skin gleamed in the bright morning light, his blond hair made even lighter by the sun. He'd invited her to swim with him, but she didn't like the water anymore, not since last summer. Not since Russell had found her in the beach house and....

She shook away the thought with a toss of her long, wavy black hair and drew her knees up, clasping her hands around her flared denims as Frank drew nearer. She picked up a towel and tossed it to him.

"Thanks," he laughed, sniffing as he mopped the

water from his face and chest. "Whew, I'm tired! Why didn't you come in with me?"

"In these?" she asked, indicating her pale blue tee shirt and jeans. Her rain-gray eyes lit up with laughter. "If there are any sharks out there, they'd die laughing. Was it cold?"

"Freezing." He pulled on a short-sleeved shirt and dropped down on the sand beside her, pushing back his unruly hair. "Having fun?" he asked with a boyish grin.

"Ummm," she murmured lazily. "It's been a wonderful week. I'm sorry it has to end."

He studied her quietly. "I love that Georgia drawl," he said.

"What does that mean?" she asked, suddenly on the defensive.

"I mean that I like that soft accent. Did I say something insulting?" he asked quickly.

She shook her head. "I'm sorry. I've taken so much ribbing at college—not just about the accent either. People seem to have the idea that farm girls go barefoot year-round and can't spell cat."

He caught her cold hand and squeezed it. "You know I wasn't making a dig at you. Besides," he added with a smile, "it's one of the biggest farms in the state that your family owns. And you're much too cultured to be mistaken for a backwoods hick, darling."

"Thank you, kind sir," she said with a smile. "It has been fun, Frank. I wish I didn't have to go home. If Baker hadn't pressured me so...."

"It's only until Christmas," he reminded her. "And Belle and I will be down in less than three weeks. We'll be neighbors."

"Bright Meadows came on the market just at the right time, didn't it?" she laughed. "It'll make a grand vacation home for you. Now, just be sure you take enough vacations...."

He leaned over and brushed her mouth with his. "You can count on it."

She turned her gaze seaward, enjoying the companionable silence that came between them. The pleasant memories of fun-filled days that finally led to skipping a semester of college to come with Frank, his mother and sister for a late holiday on the Georgia coast came to her. Frank had been so thoughtful, so kind on those dazzling New York City evenings, so gentle, not at all like that dark-eyed savage at Currie Hall....

She flushed with the vivid memory, the consuming embarrassment that had kept her away from the sprawling family farm for a full year, causing her to find excuse after excuse to avoid going home on holidays.

Russell hadn't seemed to notice or care about her conspicuous absence or about the fact that she pointedly ignored any reference to him in her infrequent letters and phone calls. But, then, nothing affected him. Nothing but the land that was his life, his passion. Always and forever, there was the land. She used to watch him, standing like some dark god in a Greek myth, gazing out over the curves of a mistress turned to sandy loam by an evil spell. It was something she couldn't understand because she hated the fertile black soil that had taken her parents.

Her eyes misted at the memory. She'd been the type of child that Frank Tyler and his kind wouldn't have noticed without a grimace of distaste. She'd been dirty, dressed in faded, worn cotton frocks; she'd always gone barefoot, with her hair constantly in tangles despite her frail mother's best efforts. And her language had been enough to raise even Russell's eyebrows. By the time she was eight, that horrible year when her father died because of a field hand's carelessness and her mother succumbed to pneumonia complicated by heartbreak, she was fire-tempered and a step short of illiterate.

Russell Currie had taken that belligerent little ragamuffin in his big, hard arms and carried her up to the big house, mastering her struggles effortlessly as she cursed him and kicked. He'd made Mattie open a room for her and dared his father and stepmother to sav a word about the decision.

"She belongs to me," he told Baker and Mindy, with fiery determination in his dark, dark eyes. "I promised her mother on her deathbed that I'd take her and by God I'll make a lady out of her if it kills us both!"

It hadn't been easy, she admitted ruefully. But Baker and Mindy had accepted her with open arms, and even baby Eileen had taken to her like a playful kitten. With Russell, it was another matter. He was a hard taskmaster, and she wore out her rebellion against the stone wall of his will. But day by day through careful work and determination, he pushed the circumstances of her father's death to the back of her mind. He bought her clothes, tutored her sharp mind and dulled her sharp tongue, and produced a reasonable facsimile of a lady in only ten short years. And he screamed bloody murder when at eighteen, Baker had taken her side when she fought Russell to go to a northern college. But for once Baker swayed his stubborn son, and Lutecia got her way with Russell—for the first and last time.

There'd been trips home that first year of college. Until last summer, until that day....

She clasped her hands around her knees, rushing her stubborn chin on the smooth denim of her flared jeans. Snob? Perhaps Frank was right. She didn't talk about her childhood, about the way she came to be taken into the wealthy environment of Currie Hall. She couldn't bear remembering. Sometimes she felt very much like the ragged, frightened child she really was beneath her tailored pink cotton blouse and expensive jeans. It was a feeling she disliked. The memory of poverty had never died and she didn't like things that reminded her of it. Things like square dancing and farming, and the land—and Russell. Because he knew better than anybody just how great her climb really was.

"I don't want to go home," she murmured into her bent knees.

"Why didn't you tell your father that when he

called?"

She shrugged. "You know Baker had a heart attack last month," she reminded him. "Mindy took him off to Miami to get him away from those horrible Appaloosas so that he could recuperate. I couldn't undo all the doctors have done by upsetting him. Anyway, he knows how Russell would handle Eileen without Mindy's influence. I don't have the excuse of going back to school since I'm registered for next January. And he really sprung it on me before I had time to think." She sighed angrily. "It was Russell's idea. I know it was!"

Frank laughed softly, shifting to lie back on the sand. "Every time you mention his name your face burns like a beacon. What's he like?"

"Russell?" Her mind fought even the memory of him. "Middle thirties, stubborn and proud, and absolutely ruthless when he wants something. Just ask anyone who has had business dealings with him," she added bitterly. "Most farmers and ranchers lose money. Russell makes money."

"Married?" he asked.

"Russell?" she cried incredulously.

Frank shook his head and smiled. "I'm beginning to regret accepting Baker's invitation to stay at your house while they finish the work at Bright Meadows."

"Don't be silly," she chided. "It's the middle of harvest, and the Great-White-Rancher will be too busy getting the crops in and buying and selling cattle to be at home much," she said, adding silently,

"I hope! Besides, you know you and Belle are welcome. Will you come?"

He stared quietly into her wide, driftwood-gray eyes. "If you really want me to."

She frowned and laughed all at once. "What kind of question is that? Of course I want you to!"

He leaned closer and brushed her lips with his in the gentle caress that had been the hallmark of their brief relationship. "Then we'll come."

She turned her eyes toward the beach house in the distance. "Well, I guess it's about time to pack. Are you sure you don't mind driving me to the airport?"

He stood up, pulling her to her feet. "I mind letting you go," he said, suddenly serious as his eyes met hers.

She laughed self-consciously and slung back her hair. "No fair," she teased. "We agreed to keep it light, no strings."

He sighed, and the corners of his lips went up reluctantly. "So you keep reminding me. All right, beautiful, let's go. They'll be waiting breakfast for us and you know how mother hates to wait."

Amen, she thought as she followed his long strides down the beach. Remembering his flattery she smiled. Not that she believed it. Her olive complexion and dark, wavy hair were good points she knew. But Lutecia did not realize the full power of her unique beauty. Her jaw had a firm, Scotch-Irish set to it, and her cheekbones were unusually high. Her nose tilted just a bit at its tip, although the full perfection of her mouth offset that impish prank of nature. But it was her figure, she thought—and without conceit—that attracted men. It was full and rounded, and her smooth skin was flawless. She flattered it with low-cut blouses and well-fitting skirts and jeans, dressing with a flair that set her apart.

Frank clasped her hand warmly. "I told you," he laughed, nodding toward the sprawling beach house ahead.

Belle Tyler was waiting on the porch, her short blonde hair wisping in the breeze, her pale blue eyes worried.

"Thank goodness!" she said in a husky, ultra-soft voice. "Mother's been having kittens all over the house, swearing that the coffee would melt metal from reheating! Where have you been?"

Frank smiled easily at his sister. "On the beach, stoning tourists," he told her tongue-in-cheek. "Why the worried look?"

"Company's coming," she returned, studying Lutecia curiously. "You never mentioned that your brother was a pilot."

Lutecia felt her heart freeze in her breast. "How did you know?" she asked, dreading the answer.

"He called a few minutes ago. He's flying down to pick you up."

She dropped her eyes to hide the confusion and panic that casual remark caused. "When?"

"He'll be here at ten. He's going to land in Augusta and drive down." Belle cocked her blonde head at the younger girl. "If your brother looks anything like he sounds...Gosh, what a voice, deep and slow and sexy!"

"He's probably overweight and bald," Frank laughed at the obvious interest in his sister's delicate face. "Just another stuffy, middle-aged bachelor."

"Is he, Lutecia?" Belle persisted.

"Frank!" Angela Tyler interrupted, sparing an answer. "Frank, come in here and eat before our bacon freezes on the plate!" She stood in the doorway like a slender, ancient statue, her cold blue eyes taking in her son and his slumping companion. "You too, dear," she said to Lutecia, and her thin lips smiled, but the smile didn't touch her frigid eyes. "You must be hungry after that long walk. Come on, children."

Belle followed her, but Frank held back, glancing apologetically at Lutecia. "She doesn't mean to be bossy," he explained. "And when she gets to know you better, she'll warm up."

Lutecia shuddered inwardly at the thought. Already Angela looked down her nose at Lutecia despite the Currie wealth that seemed to draw her into the older woman's social corridor. Not that Frank's father had been rich; only a natural aptitude for electronics and a little foresight had boosted him up the ladder of social acceptance. And Angela had started out as a typist in a secretarial pool. Of course, that was a family secret, and Angela's acquired poise and stoic dignity resisted speculation. But the old woman's past wouldn't soften her toward Lutecia if she ever found out the

13

truth.

She followed Frank into the dining room like a sleepwalker, trying not to think about what her reaction would be when Russell walked in that door. A year had passed, but it felt like yesterday. She nibbled at her food, praying that her face wouldn't betray her to Frank and his family. If there had been anywhere she could have run to, any way of avoiding this meeting, she'd have bolted like a nervous filly.

Outside she heard the distant thunder. It was like an omen, and the perfect morning dissolved into rain.

CHAPTER TWO

After the rain passed they sat on the balcony watching the dark clouds drift across the stormy waves. Suddenly the sound of an engine interrupted Belle's animated chatter.

"It's him!" Belle cried, almost knocking over a chair in her mad flight to the living-room window. The sound of a car door slamming almost covered Belle's gasp of astonishment. "Oh, mother," she breathed onto the silence. "I know what I want for Christmas!"

Angela and her son exchanged frowns as they made their way into the main room. Lutecia hung back, her heart slamming at her throat.

Belle made it to the door before any of them and rushed out onto the porch with Angela a few quiet steps behind her. Frank turned to Lutecia as a chorus of welcomes filtered through the open door.

"What's got into her?" he queried, his hand obviously indicating Belle. "You did say he was a farmer?"

Before she could answer, the door opened wide

and Russell strode into the room, and Lutecia's breath expelled in a strange rush.

The sight of him was like a body blow, like a merciless hand choking her. He stood quietly just inside the doorway, his mahogany eyes raking over her with a thoroughness that made her tremble. He towered over Belle and Angela, and no one could have mistaken him for an ordinary farmer. He'd discarded the familiar jeans for a tailored pale gray suit that hugged the hard masculine lines of his broad chest and shoulders and slender hips. His darkness was emphasized by the cream silk shirt he wore. His deeply tanned face was hard and rugged, arrogantly handsome. Beneath his jutting brow, his narrowed eyes burned like the reflection of flame on polished wood—just as secretive, and every bit as unyielding.

He pulled a cigarette from his shirt pocket and bent his head to light it with strong, brown fingers, his narrow gaze never leaving Lutecia's face. His chiseled lips tugged up at one corner in a calculating wisp of a smile.

"You might say hello," he prompted in a deep, slow drawl.

She swallowed hard. "Hello, Russell," she managed, grasping Frank's hand and holding on tight with cold, nerveless fingers. "This is Frank Tyler. Frank, Russell Currie," she added, making the introductions in a tight voice.

Frank moved forward and extended his hand. "I'm...glad to meet you, Mr. Currie," he said hesitantly, as if he wasn't quite sure. "Lutecia's told me a lot about you," he added, his puzzled glance telling her he wasn't prepared to believe a word of what she'd told him now.

Russell gripped the outstretched hand firmly, raising an eyebrow at the dark-haired girl behind Frank. "Has she?" he replied casually.

"Your sister's a darling," Belle purred up at Russell. "We've so enjoyed having her here with us."

Both Russell's eyebrows went up this time, and the amusement was plain in his eyes.

She jerked her gaze away. What good would it do to tell him that she'd given up trying to correct the impression the Tyler's had of their relationship? He wouldn't have believed it.

"How about some coffee?" Belle cooed. "Or some tea? Anything you'd like," she added with a slow, seductive lift of her eyes.

Russell's smile deepened. "I'll settle for coffee."

"It'll only take a minute!" Belle backed away and almost ran for the kitchen. Lutecia had never seen her move so fast.

"Won't you sit down, Mr. Currie?" Angela asked, patting the sofa beside her. Her icy eyes actually smiled for him. "I'm so glad to have met you at last. Lutecia told us that you farmed, but I never expected..." She bit her lip, plainly losing her cool poise for an instant. "I mean..."

Russell crossed his long legs, and his eyes caught Lutecia's. "I know exactly what you mean, Mrs. Tyler," he said with a mocking smile.

She glared at him, and for an instant the tension in the room was almost tangible. Until Belle entered the suddenly silent room with a tray of hot coffee and started firing questions right and left at Russell.

Frank perched himself on the arm of Lutecia's chair, leaning down to whisper in her ear. "Stuffy, middle-aged bachelor?" he teased. "Good Lord, he's a walking miracle of sophistication! Or was your description colored by sibling rivalry?"

She blushed. "It's the way I remember him," she mumbled miserably.

"You're afraid of him."

Her wide, panicky eyes met his. "Afraid?" she echoed. "I'm terrified!"

A shadow crossed Frank's pale face. "Stay here," he told her. "He can't make you go back."

She held on to his hand. "Can't he?" she laughed humorlessly. "Can you stop him, Frank?"

He started to speak, but a glance in Russell's direction froze the words on his lips. The older man's hard eyes were studying them with an angry scrutiny even while he listened to Angela's casual conversation.

No one, Lutecia thought irritably, ever stood up to Russell for long. All her life, it seemed, she'd been looking for a man strong enough to do that.

"I hate to cut this visit short," Russell said suddenly, his crisp tones cutting into her musings, "but I'm short on time." He glanced at his watch, a flash of gold imbedded in a nest of thick, dark hair on his muscular wrist. "I've got a buyer flying in from Dallas to discuss a cattle deal with me. Get your things together, Tish."

She rose automatically at the authority in his voice, resenting it but not resisting. The nickname was a carryover from her childhood, from days when she tagged after the tall man like a second shadow and loved him even while she fought him.

"I'll be right back," she said, pausing to brush a casual kiss against Frank's cheek as she passed him. She ignored Russell's raised eyebrow as she rushed out of the room. It was the first time she'd made any affectionate gesture towards Frank in front of the family, and she wondered just for a second why she felt the necessity.

When she came back into the living room lugging her suitcases and purse, Belle Tyler was sitting on the couch between her mother and Russell. She was so close to him that a fly couldn't have breathed in the space between them. Lutecia's jaw clenched involuntarily.

"Oh, there you are, darling, " Belle called. "I was just telling Russell how much Frank and I are looking forward to our visit."

"I hope we won't be in the way," Frank muttered.

"Not at all," Russell replied cooly. "The invitation included you, Mrs. Tyler," he reminded Angela.

"You're very kind," she replied with a smile. "But I have some business to attend to. Since my husband's death, most of the responsibility for the company falls on me, you know."

Russell acknowledged that bland statement with

a half smile, and Tish could have laughed. Woman's Lib might have swept the country, but the words weren't included in Russell's autocratic vocabulary.

He bent to take the suitcases out of Tish's hands effortlessly, his eyes meeting hers at point-blank range with the action. "Nervous, honey?" he asked in a voice that reached only her ears, and she knew the smile would be there before she saw it.

"Because of you?" she said with a forced laugh. "How ridiculous."

"You've been clinging to Tyler like a lifeline since the minute I walked in the door," he remarked, straightening as he turned toward the door.

She said her good-byes, said all the polite, necessary things, while Russell put her bags in the trunk of his rented car. Her hand trembled under the pressure of Frank's as he led her to the passenger side.

"Cheer up," he murmured in her ear. "He is your brother, after all, and blood's thicker than water. I'll be there in two weeks. Think about that."

"I'll live on that," she corrected, and lifted her face for his brief, gentle kiss.

"Let's go," Russell said impatiently, sliding in behind the wheel, oblivious to Belle's possessive gaze.

She got in beside him and they drove away, the chorus of good-byes ringing in her ears.

Later, gliding along the highway, she felt Russell's eyes on her. "What, exactly, were they expecting,

Tish?" he asked quietly. "A gangly hayseed wearing torn jeans and carrying a pitchfork?"

She studied her hands in her lap. "You didn't disappoint Belle, at least." She threw him a glance. "She did everything but wear a sign saying 'take me, I'm yours.' "

"The line forms to the right, baby," he said absently, lighting a cigarette without taking his eyes from the road. "I'm up to my ears in women as it is."

"You always were," she said impulsively, flushing as the words died on the air. "Drawn like flies by the scent of money," she added quickly.

"In other words, my only attraction is the size of my wallet?" he asked with a hint of a smile.

"How would I know?" she asked defensively.

"How, indeed?" Soft laughter filled the car. "I'm your 'brother,' I believe?"

She flushed to the roots of her hair. "They just assumed that you were. I tried to tell them, but..."

"Like hell you did."

She folded her arms tightly across her chest and stared out the window. "What do you think of Frank?" she asked casually.

"Nice boy. What does he do for a living?"

"He isn't a boy!" she snapped.

She felt his fiery glance. "Compared to me, he is. I've got at least nine years on him."

"He's twenty-six."

"Eight years, then. I asked you a question."

"He's a vice-president in his father's company. They're in electronics."

"Well," he said, "he's pretty."

"So are you," she flashed, lifting her stubborn chin. "Pretty irritating and pretty apt to stay that way!"

She felt the fiery glance he shot in her direction, and almost shuddered at the intensity of it.

"I'll tell you once," he said in a deceptively gentle tone, "to take that chip off your shoulder. There's a line you don't cross with me, honey."

Her lip trembled with mingled antagonism and fear. "I'm almost twenty-one, Russell," she said finally. "I don't like being treated like a child. You've walked all over me since I was in grammar school, and I don't have to take it anymore."

"Don't kid yourself," he said deeply, and a wisp of smoke drifted past her as he exhaled. "You'll take anything I dish out and like it. Won't you?" he demanded harshly.

She cringed mentally at the threat in the soft tones that were a thousand times worse than shouting. "You started it," she mumbled tearfully. "You were mad when you got to the beach house, and you're still mad. Must you be so cruel, Russell?"

"Baby, you don't know how cruel I can be," he said matter-of-factly. "And if you don't take the edge off that sharp little tongue, I'll show you."

She drew in a deep breath, blinking back the tears. "I'm sorry," she said finally, almost choking on her pride with the words.

They were in the city now, and he stopped for a traffic light, throwing a lazy arm over the back of the seat. His eyes scanned her drawn face, and she reluctantly returned his gaze.

His fingers caught a loose strand of her hair and tugged at it. "That was a hell of a welcome," he said roughly, "for a man you haven't seen in a year."

"Has it been that long?" she asked innocently.

"You know damned well it has. And you haven't stopped running yet, have you?" His eyes bit into hers with a vengeance.

"I don't want to talk about it," she said shakily, her hand going to his, trying to loose it from her hair.

He caught her fingers in his big, warm hand, and the touch was electric, jolting. "I didn't mean to be quite so brutal," he said quietly, his eyes searching hers. "And I sure as hell didn't expect to find you gone, bag and baggage, before I had time to explain."

Her fingers went cold in his, and she could feel something inside her melting, aching. She tugged at the firm clasp and he released her as he moved the car back into traffic.

"My God," he said roughly, "the way you'd been flirting with every man on the place, including me," he added with a challenging glance, "what did you expect me to think? There you were in the bath house, in Jimmy Martin's arms, and you were wearing nothing but a towel! He was damned lucky I didn't kill him."

She closed her eyes against the memory. She could still see Russell's eyes the way they'd looked that day, blazing, merciless, as he literally threw Jimmy out the door.

Like the boy he was, Jim ran for his life, leaving Lutecia there to bear the brunt of Russell's black temper, the searing accusations, and what had followed....

"You might have told me about the rattlesnake to begin with," Russell said, turning the car into the road that led to the nearby airport.

"You wouldn't have listened," she said in a husky whisper. "It was curled up in my clothes, and I didn't even see it until I'd taken off my swimsuit. I grabbed the towel, and screamed...."

"And Martin just happened to be riding around the lake. I know, damn it." His jaw tightened in profile. "Mindy said you phoned her to bring you some more clothes. By the time I cooled down and came home, you were long gone. You wouldn't even answer your damned phone at college!"

"I never wanted to see you or talk to you again," she murmured, turning her eyes to the parking lot ahead.

"So your roommate told me." He pulled the car into a parking space at the airport terminal and cut the engine. His dark eyes narrowed on her face, traveling down to her plunging neckline and remaining there so intently that she folded her arms self-consciously over the gap.

Was he remembering, too, she wondered? Remembering what had happened after Jimmy Martin ran away?

She could still hear Russell's voice, the quiet fury in it that cut like tiny whips as he'd dragged her trembling body in the damp towel wholly into his arms.

"My God, you've been begging for this all summer," he'd growled, holding her mercilessly even as she struggled, "why fight me now?"

And he'd bent his head. And even now, a year later, she could still feel the hard, cruel pressure of his mouth as it took hers, the humiliation of a kiss without tenderness or consideration or warmth. It had been, as he meant it, a punishment to hurt her pride as much as her soft mouth. When he'd finished and she was shaking like a leaf from the shock of it, he'd thrown her away from him. And the words he'd used to describe her as he strode out of the bath house had left her crying and had sent her running from Currie Hall before he came home.

She swallowed nervously, avoiding his intent gaze.

"I couldn't forget," she whispered, "what you called me. It wasn't true, any of it, and...!"

"I know." His big hand touched her cheek, gently. The back of his fingers were cool against the heated flesh. "God, Tish, we were so close! I knew better, even when I accused you, but the sight of you and Martin...I lost my head. I wanted to hurt you, and that was the only thing on my mind."

Unconsciously her lips trembled. "You succeeded."

His fingers touched that full, soft mouth lightly.

25

"I know. I could feel your mouth trembling under mine."

Her face went scarlet at the words. Until that day, she and Russell had been like brother and sister. She'd followed him everywhere as an adolescent. Even when he went to dull livestock auctions, she endured the smell of cattle and horses and sweat and smoke just to be near him.

It had been like that all through school; she had bragged about her bigger-than-life adopted brother to the other children when they teased her about being a sharecropper's daughter. Even though Russell had bought her new clothes, the children remembered the flour-sack dresses she once had worn, and threw it up to her. All she had to do was threaten them with Russell, and knowing his temper, they'd shut up. But that was childhood. And now, she wasn't a 'sister' anymore...

"A year," Russell remarked absently, "and you're still terrified of me."

She swallowed down a hasty denial and brushed at a stray lock of dark hair. "Please," she said quietly. "I don't want to talk about it."

He lit a cigarette and sat smoking it until the silence decended on them like a fog. "It's damned hard to face a problem by walking away from it, Tish," he said finally.

Her chin lifted proudly. "I don't have any problems."

"Thank you for that stoic testimony, Saint Joan, and shall we both pray for rain before the flames hit you?"

Her face became a bright red and the laughter welled up inside her and burst like a summer storm. Russell's dark eyes glittered with amusement, and the years fell away. Quite suddenly, the antagonism she'd felt was gone like a shadow before sunlight.

"Oh, Russell, you...!" she cried, exasperated.

Chuckling, he crushed out his cigarette. "Come on, brat. Let's go home."

Minutes later, she was sitting in the cockpit of Russell's Cessna Skyhawk while he went over the preflight checklist, a procedure that was still incomprehensible to her.

She watched him with quiet, caressing eyes and saw the way the light burned in his dark hair. Despite the events of the past year, the dreams she had always had about him had never really stopped. The vague longing persisted. The look that had flashed through his stormy eyes that lazy summer afternoon when the whole pattern of her life seemed abruptly to change forever still haunted her.

Anyway, she had Frank. Frank, who was younger and handsomer and so undemanding. Frank, who wouldn't remind her of the childhood that had caused so many nightmares.

But, oddly, she wanted Currie Hall again. She wanted Mattie, little and wiry and coffee-colored, to call her 'sugar cane' and fuss over her. She wanted old Joby's lazy smile as he polished the silver and hummed spirituals in the kitchen while Mattie cooked. She wanted Eileen's gay laughter and the feel of the towering old house nestled among the pecan trees that were old enough to remember Reconstruction and the ragged trail of weary Confederate soldiers making their way home.

How was it possible to love something and hate it all at once, she wondered, and again her eyes were drawn to Russell as he eased his formidable weight into the plane beside her.

He tossed the clipboard with the checklist onto the back seat of the four-seater plane and threw a grin at Tish. "Ready?" he asked.

"Ready." She checked her seat belt and her door while he cleared the plane for takeoff and taxied out onto the runway to wait for the final go-ahead.

When it came and he pulled back on the throttle, she felt a rush of excitement as the small craft gathered speed and nosed up toward the sky in a smooth, breathless rush.

Russell chuckled at the wild pleasure in her face. "It wasn't me you missed," he taunted. "It was the damned airplane."

"I love it!" she cried above the drone of the engine.

"Do you? I'll wait until we get over some open country and treat you to a few barrel rolls," he mused.

"You wouldn't!" she gasped, gripping the seat.

He caught the expression in her eyes and threw back his head, laughing like the devil he was.

"Russell Currie, if you dare turn this plane over

with me in it, I'll...I'll send an anonymous letter to the Federal Aviation Administration!" she sputtered.

"Baby, there isn't much I wouldn't dare, and you know it," he replied. "All right, calm down. We'll save the stunts for another time."

She glanced at him apprehensively. The lion was content now, his dark eyes bright with the pleasure of soaring above the crowded expressways, of challenging the clouds.

She wondered if he was remembering other flights. In Vietnam he had been a combat pilot and she and the rest of the family had lived for letters and rare trans-Atlantic phone calls, and the six o'clock news had held a terrifying fascination with its daily reports on offensives and skirmishes. He'd been wounded in an attack on the base and spent weeks in a hospital in Hawaii. When he finally came home there was death in his eyes, and he had bouts with alcohol that threatened to last forever. It was rumored that his problems were caused, not by a winnerless war but by the death of a dark-haired woman in childbirth. A woman, the only woman, Russell had ever loved. It was a subject no one, not even Baker, dared to discuss with Russell Currie. A subject Tish only knew about from vaguely remembered bits and pieces of overheard conversation.

She studied his profile with a tiny frown. His reputation with women was enough to make protective mothers blanch, but, somehow, she avoided thinking of him in that respect. It was too dangerous to remember how those hard arms had felt in an embrace, how that firm, chiseled mouth...

He turned suddenly and caught her curious stare. It was as though those piercing dark eyes could see the thoughts in her mind. One dark eyebrow went up as his gaze dropped relentlessly to the soft curve of her mouth and lingered there until her cheeks flushed red, and she jerked her face toward the window.

Soft laughter merged with the sound of the engine. She closed her eyes against it.

It only seemed like minutes before the sprawling town square of Ashton came into view below, like an oasis of civilization surrounded by miles and miles of farmland.

Tish smiled unconsciously, gazing down on the growing metropolis that had sprung from the major economic base of agriculture. Ashton was an old city with its roots in the Confederacy and its veneer of progress spread thin over prejudices that ran deep.

Like all southern cities, it had that sultry atmosphere of leisure and courtesy that endeared it to the natives while annoying the hell out of impatient northern tourists. The surrounding countryside was an artist's vision of green perfection, from gently thrusting hillside to groves of pecan and oak trees nestled between new industry and old architecture.

Churches lined the wide, heavily traveled streets. They were predominatly Baptist and rabidly outspoken every time the liquor referendum was revived. Republicans were rumored to live in the community, but the Democrats beat them so bloody at the polls that most of them were reluctant to admit their political affiliation. Troublemakers were dealt with quickly and efficiently, and not always by law enforcement personnel. In fact, Sheriff Blakely—who had been sheriff for so long, few locals could remember when he wasn't—had been known to run the State Patrol and FBI agents out of his jurisdiction when they interfered with his authority. Creek County had a formidable reputation for taking care of its own, in spite of state government.

Tish smiled, lost in her musings. With all its faults and vices, this was home country—Georgia. The beginning and end of her world, whether she wanted it that way or not. In this pocket of the largest state east of the Mississippi River, she could trace her ancestry back almost a hundred and fifty years— generations of farmers...

The word was enough to turn her thoughts black. Farming. Her father, that horrible inhuman scream...

"No!" The word broke from her involuntarily.

"What is it, baby?" Russell asked quickly, glancing at her with concern.

She drew a sharp breath, banishing the memory again. "Nothing. Nothing at all." She leaned back against the seat and let her eyelids fall.

He set the plane down in a perfect three-point landing on the private airstrip at Currie Hall, and her heart began to race wildly as she caught a glimpse of the house, far in the distance, half-hidden in the green curtain of towering oaks and pecan trees.

Beyond the airstrip, the fields were covered with green growth that had to be peanuts or soybeans, she knew by their proximity to the ground. But they weren't the dark green they should have been, and she looked up at Russell with a question in her eyes.

"Drought," he said, answering it as he answered most of her unasked questions, as if he could sometimes read her mind. "It's been a long hot spell, and I've had to replant most of the corn. To make matters worse, the armyworms came this month. We're going to take a hell of a licking financially before I straighten this mess out. It's causing problems with the cattle too," he added, shutting down the engine with a sharp jerk of his lean fingers. "We won't have enough silage for the winter, and that means more money for feed this year. It's the same over most of the stae. A hell of a bad year."

"You'll sell off most of the cattle, I guess?" she asked absently.

He nodded. "Either that or try to feed them, and we'll lose our shirts either way." He eyed her curiously. "You haven't forgotten as much as I'd thought, even though you've been buried in concrete for two years. I'd almost believe you've been reading the market bulletins."

"Baker sent me a subscription to the local paper," she said smugly. "I even know about the corn fungus that's poisoning the crop for cattle."

"God!" he exclaimed with reluctant admiration. "You'll make some farmer a wife, yet."

She glowered at him. "I told you years ago I'd never marry a farmer," she reminded him. "I'd rather die than be buried in the country for the rest of my life."

His eyes narrowed on her face. "If you were a few years older, I might change your mind about that. When are you going to stop burying your head in the sand? You can't run away, baby."

"What am I running from?" she asked, her full lips tightening as she glared up at him.

"The past, your childhood—me," he added with a strange half-smile.

The look in his eyes knocked the breath out of her. She opened the door of the plane and stepped down onto the hot pavement, sweeping her hair back with a restless hand.

The jeep was sitting on the edge of the strip where he'd left it and she started toward it. When he got there with her suitcases, she was waiting for him in the front seat. She eyed the thin layer of dust on the seat with distaste.

"I can remember a little girl who didn't mind dust," he remarked as he got in under the wheel.

"I'm not a little girl anymore," she returned.

crossing her legs as she began to feel the smothering fury of the sun.

She felt his eyes on her in a patient yet intense gaze. "God, don't I know it?" he murmured deeply.

Nervously, her eyes crawled sideways to meet that searching gaze, and a shudder of excitement ran through her.

Abruptly Russell turned away and started the engine. "Oh, hell, let's get out of here. The damned sun's frying me," he growled, and the jeep shot forward.

"How's Baker, Russell?" she asked as they drove down the long, yellow dust road to the farm, where sleek horses grazed in the once-green meadows, their spotted flanks proclaiming them to be Appaloosas.

"Healing," he said. "Slowly," he added with a glimmer of a smile. "Mindy's keeping him away from horses in West Palm Beach, but it'll be hell driving him away from the stables when he comes home."

"When will that be?"

"Christmas, of course. That's why you're here," he added, leaning over to crush out his finished cigarette in the ashtray. "I can't manage the farm and Eileen at the same time with harvest staring me in the face."

"Is that all?" she asked curiously.

He glowered at her. "No, that's not all. There's a boy."

Her eyebrows went up and she grinned

mischievously. "Oh, glory, I've always wanted to be a professional chaperone! Next to bathing pigs for a living, it's what I love best."

He chuckled, shaking his head as he pulled into the driveway. "Damned brat, how have I done without you?"

She tossed her long hair. "Poorly, Mr. Currie, poorly," she said, turning her attention to the wide expanse of land with its fringe of trees far on the horizon. Looming up ahead was the towering white house its square columns and pure lines as elegant as the stately oaks and pecan trees surrounding it. Mattie was waiting on the long, spacious porch when Russell pulled up at the steps. Tish ran into the old woman's thin, wiry arms with a cry of pleasure.

The slender little black woman held her tight, bending her gray head over Tish's shoulder. "Lordy, I'd forgot how pretty you are, sugar cane," she laughed. "It's good to have you home again!"

"It's good to be home again," she murmured, her eyes searching the porch and finding the same swing she sat in as a child, the big rocker where Russell used to hold her and rock her late in the evening as the family sat here.

Joby came through the door. He looked a little more stooped in his walk than before but was still proud, even in his advancing age. Grinning from ear to ear, he took Tish's outstretched hand and held it warmly between both of his.

"Welcome home, Miss Tish," he said. "It sho' will be good to have you here. Miss Eileen don't make enough noise to liven this old place up."

"I wouldn't take bets, if I were you," Russell said darkly. "Two more hours of that hard rock last night, and I'd have pulled the fusebox. Damned tape player could wake the dead."

"She's only seventeen, Russell," Tish protested.

"That's the same thing Baker used to tell me about you, and I didn't buy it then either, did I?" he taunted.

She glowered up at him, noticing the dark tan that gave him a vaguely foreign look, the whipcord slimness that hallmarked a body as tough as leather, the broad shoulders and hard chest that once pillowed a little girl's head. A sensuous aura of masculinity cloaked him, and suddenly she felt like running.

"You're a tyrant, you know," she told him, hiding her fear in antagonism.

"And you're a little insurrectionist," he said with a slow, lazy smile. His eyes, narrowed to slits, glittered down at her. "Exercising your claws on me, kitten?"

"Must you patronize me, Russell?" she shot back.

"You better call over at Miss Nan's," Mattie said quickly, stepping between them, "and tell Eileen you're here. In all the excitement, I just plain forgot to tell you she wasn't home."

"I'll surprise her instead," Tish said. She glanced at Russell, who was standing quietly with a smoking cigarette in his hand, just watching her. "Can I borrow your car?" she asked.

"Hell, no."

A tiny smile tugged at her lips. "I do wish you could just give me a straight answer," she said.

Once he would have smiled at that, but his face was as smooth as glass. The only expression was in his narrowed eyes, and it made her ankles melt.

"Flirting gets you nothing from me," he said grimly, "or doesn't your memory stretch that far?"

She blushed to her heels. Behind her, Mattie mumbled, "Here we go again," and Joby headed for the kitchen.

"I wasn't..." she protested.

"While you're upstairs," he went on relentlessly, his eyes sweeping to the exposed curve of her full breasts, "put on another blouse. That getup may be suitable for a resort beach, but you're a long way from the ocean now."

"Took the words right out of my mouth," Mattie murmured, quickly heading out behind Joby when she caught the flash of fire in Tish's wide gray eyes.

"Russell Currie, I won't...!" she started.

"Shut up." The words were very quietly spoken. He didn't raise his voice. The look in his eyes was enough. She'd seen him stop fights between the fieldhands with it without ever saying a word.

"We'd better understand each other from the start," he said quietly. "Playing is one thing, I enjoy it as much as you do. But flirting is something else. Save it for Tyler. I don't want any repeats of last summer."

Her lips trembled with suppressed fury. "Neither do I," she said with as much cold dignity as she could muster, raising her chin proudly. "And I wasn't flirting. You accused me of having a chip on my shoulder, but I think it's the other way around, Russell."

He took a long draw from the cigarette. "You just keep an eye on Eileen, baby girl, and save the come-get-me glances for boys your own age. You ought to know by now that it's all or nothing with me—in everything."

She straightened, turning away from him to the staircase. "I haven't been home ten minutes, and you're jumping to conclusions all over again," she said icily. "All right, Russell, if it's war, it's war. I'll keep out of your way."

"Get your clothes changed. I'll run you over to Nan's."

She froze with her back to him. "I'd rather...couldn't Joby drive me?"

"Ten minutes," he said, turning on his heel.

The trouble with arguing with Russell, she fumed while she exchanged her beachwear for a pair of white slacks and a high crewneck patterned brown and white blouse, was that he wouldn't argue. He said what he wanted to, ignored what anyone else said, and walked off. Flirting, he accused. Was it flirting to kid with him? She jerked a brush through her wavy hair enthusiastically. Her face stony in the mirror. If she could only hold on until Frank came south, at least she'd have an ally. She paused and smiled. No, Nan and Eileen would do for now. She sighed. She had friends, after all.

He was waiting impatiently in the hall when she got downstairs, two minutes under the deadline. In the tailored brown denim jeans and khaki work shirt, he looked even taller, more imposing, than the suit he had been wearing. He eyed her carelessly, his eyes shadowed by the brim of his ranch hat, which sat at a rakish angle over his jutting brow.

"Little sophisticate," he chided, his eyes taking her in from the white Italian sandals to the white band that held her hair back. "Who are you trying to impress?"

The sarcasm in his deep, lazy voice flicked her like a silver-tipped whip.

"Not you, for a fact," she returned, keeping her temper in check.

He only smiled, but there was no humor in it. "Let's go."

He put her in the jeep beside him and backed it out to the side of the garage.

She shifted uncomfortably, aware of the traces of red dust that were going to cling to those crisp white slacks if she so much as breathed the wrong way.

"Want to change into something darker?" he asked.

"How about the Lincoln?" she returned sharply.

"I work, Miss Priss," he replied as he pulled into the driveway and started down it with a jerk as he shifted the gear in the floorboard. His hand was dangerously near her leg, and she moved closer to the door. "The Lincoln looks a little showy to take digging post holes with me," he finished without even a glance betraying that he'd seen her slide away.

She shrugged, turning her head to watch the rolling, soft swell of the land, green and sweet smelling in the afternoon breeze. They passed the Appaloosas again, and she grimaced when she saw them. That wild streak in Baker Russell wouldn't let him rest until he finished whatever he started, and that included breaking one stubborn Appaloosa stallion. It had caused him to have a heart attack, yet he was still restless to get back to his horses. He'd said as much to Tish over the phone.

Her eyes glanced at Russell, sitting easily in the seat with his hat cocked over one eye, his face impassive. That same wildness was in him, she thought, involuntarily studying the sharp masculine profile, her eyes lingering on the strong, brown hands on the steering wheel. Russell would break before he would let anything bend him—especially a woman.

In a shady spot on the winding, sandy road, he suddenly pulled the jeep onto the flat shoulder under a bushy chinaberry tree and cut the engine. The sounds of machinery in the distance sawed into the quiet of the nearby forest, a quiet which usually was broken only by the intermittent chirp of crickets, the warble of songbirds. It was, Tish thought, impossibly far from the watery roar of the sea and the cry of gulls, so far from the sounds of freeway traffic and blaring horns and city noises. Involuntarily, she relaxed against the seat and closed her eyes with a smile.

"Country girl," Russell said gently, his big hand brushing at a yellowjacket as it tried to land on her bare arm. "Fight it all you can, baby, but your heart's here, just as much as mine is."

She turned her head on the seat and met his teasing gaze. Remembering his dark, sudden anger, she couldn't smile the hurt away. "Are you leading up to another lecture about fast city men and slow Southern girls and the advantages of life in the country?" she asked cooly. "You can't seem to manage a civil word for me unless there's a sermon tacked onto it."

"Stop that." He pushed the brim of his hat back and stared across the fields where bare-chested field hands were just beginning to slow down in the heat, ready for frosty cans of cold beer as they left the tractors in between the rows of hay they were raking and bunching into bale. The green and yellow tractors were colorful against the horizon.

"Don't you ever get tired, Tish," he asked harshly, "of pretending to be something you're not?"

"I'm not pretending," she returned icily, folding her arms across her chest as though she felt a chill.

"Aren't you?" He turned in the seat, lighting a cigarette while he stared at her. He let out a stream of gray smoke. "Honest poverty is nothing to be ashamed of. Your father..."

"Please!" the word broke involuntarily from her

41

lips, and she bowed her head, her teeth catching her lower lip, her eyes closed. "Please, don't!"

He sighed heavily. "My God, can't you talk about it yet, after all these years? Bottling it up inside you..."

"Please!" she repeated huskily.

"All right, damn it, all right!" He scowled down at her, something restless and wild in the look his dark eyes gave her. "God, baby, don't. Don't suffer so."

She shook back her hair and the tears, and lifted her face to the breeze. "Can we go? I want to see Eileen and Nan."

"Does Tyler know the truth?" he growled suddenly. "Does he know what you crawled up from? Does he care?"

A tremor went through her. "You wouldn't dare tell him...!" she cried, as if he'd hit her.

His face was impassive, but something flashed in his narrowed eyes. "You can't run from yourself," he said.

She wanted to hit him, to hurt him. "I remember, Russell, is that what you want?" she asked huskily, fighting tears. "I remember dresses made out of flour sacks, and shoes that were too big because they were so cheap; and the other kids laughing at me because I had nothing...nothing! But I did have my pride, and I never let them see how much it hurt!" Her eyes widened, aching, burning with the memory. "Even when you brought me here and put new clothes on me and bought me shoes that fit, it changed nothing! I was that sharecropper's brat, and nobody wanted anything to do with me because I was white trash! Thank you, I remember it very well!"

"You remember all the wrong things," he said quietly, his hand reaching out to brush one lone tear from her silky cheek. "I remember that you never shirked your chores, or told lies, or asked for anything. All those years, Tish, and you never asked for a single thing. Did you have so much?"

She looked into her lap. "I had you, Russell," she whispered. "You were my best friend...then."

"And now I'm your worst enemy, is that it?" He brushed back the hair from her temple.

"That's it," she replied stonily.

He drew his hand back and started the jeep.

Minutes later, the brakes squealed as Russell pulled up in front of the ancient Coleman home. Tish smiled at the familiar lines of the pre-Civil War architecture. It was white, and had two stories and square columns. It was outrageously conventional, like Jace Coleman himself, with no frills or elegant carving on the woodwork. It was austerely simple in its lines and was practical right down to the front porch that ran the width of the house and held a porch swing and a smattering of old, but comfortable, rocking chairs and pots of flowers that bloomed every spring.

As Tish got out of the jeep, ignoring Russell's watchful gaze, the sound of feminine voices burst out of the house.

"You're back, you're really back!" A small, plump whirlwind with short black hair came bounding out the front porch and down the steps, almost knocking Tish down as she was caught around the neck by small hands and soundly hugged.

"Lena!" she murmured, hugging the younger girl as the pet name of childhood caught her unawares. "Oh, I missed you so!"

"No kidding? With that blond-haired, blue-eyed dreamboat you told me about sitting at your feet, and you missed *me?* Come on, Tish!" Eileen laughed, a flash of perfect white teeth in a face dominated by big dark eyes. "But I sure have missed you. You don't know what a *beast* Russell's been to live with lately!"

"Surely, you jest," Tish teased, with a hard glance at the towering man beside the jeep that told him it was no joke to her.

"That one didn't fly over my head, baby," Russell cautioned with a sharp smile. "Careful."

"They're at it again, I see," Nan Coleman sighed from the porch, eyeing Russell and Tish. "Fighting, and Tish hasn't been home an hour."

"Forty-five minutes," she replied, laughing as she went to hug the dainty brunette on the steps. She looked into curious green eyes. "I came right over. How are you, Nan?"

"Bored to tears," the shorter woman wailed, cutting her eyes provocatively to Russell. "All the handsome men in the county are busy with harvest."

"I thought I made up for that before harvest,"

44

Russell said, his voice deep and sensuous as he smiled, his eyes holding Nan's until she blushed.

Tish felt a sudden emptiness inside her and turned quickly to Eileen. "I brought you a present from the coast," she said, with a lightness in her voice that was a direct contrast to the dead weight of her heart. "A coral necklace."

"When did you find the time to shop?" Eileen laughed.

"I managed a few minutes away from Frank."

"Tell me about him," Nan said, taking her arm. "I've never known you get serious about a man. He must be special."

"Nan will bring us home, Russell," Eileen called over her shoulder. "Tell Mattie we'll be back before supper, okay?"

"Okay, brat," he told his sister.

Nan stopped and turned. "Oh, Russ, I'm having a party for Tish next Saturday night, kind of a homecoming get-together. You'll come, too?"

He lifted a dark eyebrow, but his eyes danced. "I might."

"He may not come for you," Eileen told Nan, "but he'll come for his 'baby,' " she added with a mischievous wink at Tish.

"I'm not anybody's baby," Tish said quietly. "I'm almost twenty-one, Eileen."

"Makes no difference," Nan said from her five years advantage. "Paternal fondness doesn't recognize age, does it, Russell?"

His dark eyes swept over Tish's face, and she

fought a blush at the intensity of it. He climbed into the jeep.

"Will you come?" Nan persisted.

"Maybe." He turned the jeep and drove away without a backward glance.

"Maybe!" Nan groaned, standing with her hands on her small hips as she watched him roar away in a cloud of dust. "That," she said, "is the most exasperating man God ever made! Just when you think you've got him in the palm of your little hand, he flies away with your fingers."

"You knew better," Eileen teased. "Russell belongs to Lisa, and no woman stands a chance against her."

Tish started to ask about Lisa—there was something familiar about the name, as if she'd heard it before at Currie Hall—but Nan was already talking again.

"...never seen him so restless," she was saying as they went inside.

"I don't know what's wrong," Eileen sighed. "He's been like a caged tiger for the past couple of weeks. It's the crops, I guess. This had been a rotten year for farming."

"Tell me about it," Nan laughed. "You ought to hear Dad when he gets the market reports. But let's not talk about crops. I want to hear all about Tish's trip."

"I want to hear all about Frank Tyler," Eileen said, dropping down beside Tish on the Early American sofa in the parlor while Nan went for iced tea. "What does he do?"

"He's an electronics engineer. His family owns an electronics company, and he's a vice-president," she said.

"Oh," Eileen said.

"But, he's wonderful," Tish protested, crestfallen at her adopted sister's reaction. "Good looking, talented; he doesn't even have to work, he just enjoys doing it."

"So does Russell," Eileen said. "Fourteen and sixteen hours a day sometimes."

"Eileen, I'm not comparing them," Tish said pointedly. "We both know Russell's a breed apart from any other man. But I like Frank very much. I think you'll like him, too."

"Can he ride?" Eileen asked.

"I don't know."

"Does he hunt or fish?"

Tish cleared her throat. "What are you going to wear to Nan's party, Lena?" she asked, hoping to divert the younger girl.

"A gag, if she doesn't shut up," Nan laughed, bringing in a tray with three frosty glasses of iced tea in cut crystal glasses on it.

"Amen," Tish said with a smile. She took a glass and drank thirstily. "Just what have you got against Frank, seeing you don't even know him?" Tish asked Eileen.

The teenager's full lips pouted. "He's a Yankee."

"Oh, for God's sake, you sound just like Russell," Nan said, shaking her head. "Even though he was championing civil rights before it was even popular, he has that one abiding prejudice."

"Me, too," Eileen said ungrammatically. "They don't belong. They come in and buy up land as if they're buying up a heritage with it, and they think owning one acre gives them the right to rebuild their neighbors in their own images.

"Hark, hear the voice of wisdom calling yonder," Tish said, cupping her hand over her ear. She ducked as Eileen, laughing, drew back her glass as if to throw it.

"Lena, you're impossible," Tish smiled.

"Russ says it's my middle name," Eileen agreed. "Oh, Tish, make him let me go to the party with Gus. He'll do it if you ask him."

"Huh?"

"Gus. Gus Hamack. You remember him, he had red hair and two teeth missing and I used to take him apples to school," Eileen prodded her memory. She smiled. "Of course, he has all his teeth now, and he's over six feet and just gorgeous! He's at Jeremiah Blakely college studying to be a soil conservationist, and Russ lets him work here every other quarter so he can pay his tuition. Please, Tish?"

"We'll see," Tish replied uncertainly, her heart freezing just at the thought of facing another battle with Russell.

"I'm going to wear something real slinky," Eileen went on as if the whole matter was settled, leaning toward Tish with the excitement burning like brown coals in her eyes. "I'll show it to you when we get home. It's blue and clingy, and off the shoulder, and if I wear a heavy wrap I may get out of the house before Russell makes me change."

Tish shook her head in defeat. "Now I know what I've missed most," she laughed.

It was late afternoon when Nan dropped Tish and Eileen off at Currie Hall. Mattie insisted on fixing her usual gigantic supper, even though the girls protested a lack of appetite. Tish wore a casual light blue shirtwaist dress to the table, a carryover from childhood when Baker Russell refused to allow a pair of feminine legs in pants to sit near him. Schooled as her nerves were, though, they still shivered when she caught Russell's mocking gaze as she sat down next to Eileen.

"Has Dwight Haley already left?" Eileen asked while they ate.

Russell nodded. "He had to get back to Dallas. He bought your Angus bull," he told the young girl with a half smile.

"Big Ben?" Eileen wailed. "Gosh, Russ, I raised him from a nubbin, and he was the only Angus for miles and miles. Everybody's got Herefords," she grumbled.

"That's why you haven't got Big Ben anymore," he replied cooly, sipping his coffee and grimacing at the scalding taste. He set the cup down. "I couldn't risk having him get in with my breeding stock. I'll let you have one of the Hereford calves to pet."

"Sure, Russ, you'll let me have it to pet until it gets

200 pounds on it," she groaned, "and then one night I'll find out I'm eating it for supper. That's cruel."

"Cruelty can be a kindness, kitten," he said abstractedly as he glanced at Tish, who quickly dropped her gaze to a mound of mashed potatoes and gravy.

"How would you like it if I sold one of your old Apps without telling you first?" Eileen was still grumbling.

"Depends."

"On what?"

"On how much you got for him," Russell grinned.

"Oh, Russ," Eileen said, capitulating with a smile.

Tish watched the byplay between brother and sister while she savored the taste of her steak and onions. Russell was so good to look at, she thought. Had that arrogant tilt of his head always been so attractive, and why hadn't she ever noticed the way his dark hair curled just a little at the ends where it lay against his muscular neck? Her eyes traveled to his profile, chiseled and commanding in that dark face, his nose straight, his brow jutting, his jaw square and stubborn...

His head turned suddenly, his dark eyes narrowing, glittering, under a black scowl when he caught her eyes on him. She quickly dropped her gaze to her plate and hated the sudden heat in her cheeks.

Pushing back her far-from-empty plate, she rose. "I'm going to sit on the porch for a while," she said, leaving before anyone could ask why she hadn't finished her supper.

She almost ran for the sanctuary of the long, wide porch, vaguely aware of the soft, deep laughter behind her.

She plopped down in the comfortable porch swing and rocked it into motion, listening to the sound of hounds baying mournfully in the distance, the sound of crickets closer at hand. Her heart was slamming at her ribs from that fiery encounter with Russell's eyes. She crossed her arms across her breasts, feeling a sudden sweet chill with the memory. Frank has blond hair, she told herself, and blue eyes, and I can have him if I want him.

"Tish!" Eileen called suddenly, breaking in on the solitude with all the tact of an atom bomb.

"Over here, Lena!"

The younger girl scurried around the corner and sat down on the edge of the settee. "Russ's coming out," she said quickly. "You won't forget to ask him about Gus, will you?"

The remembered question made her blood run hot. She knew, quite suddenly, that she didn't want to be alone with him. "Stay here," she told Eileen, "we'll ask him together."

"Oh, no you don't," Eileen protested, jumping up. "He'd eat me alive if he knew I asked you. Please, Tish, I'll do you a favor someday. Please?"

She gave in. It was impossible not to, with those great, dark eyes pleading eloquently in the warm light of the window beside the swing.

"All right, I'll ask him."

Impulsively, Eileen bent and hugged her. "You're the best sister anyone could want, even if you aren't really my sister. Thanks!"

She turned and ran toward the door, almost colliding with Russell, and gasped.

"Gosh, Russ, do you have to stalk people?" she exclaimed. "You're as big as a house!"

"Two more helpings of apple cobbler," he reminded the young girl, his voice deep and slow, "and that description may fit you too."

"I was only planning on having one," she argued. "Well, I'm going up to my room. Tomorrow's a school day, and I've still got homework to do."

"No TV until it's done," Russell called after her.

"Yes, Sir!" Eileen called cheekily, and ran for her life.

Russell eased his tall frame into the settee and leaned back to light a cigarette. He was away from the window and all Tish could see of him was the red tip of the cigarette as her eyes slowly became accustomed to the dark.

"The answer is no," he told her.

"To what?" she replied, hoping her voice sounded calm.

"Whatever Lena tried to bribe you into asking me. Something to do with Gus, no doubt," he said as he rocked the settee into motion.

"She wants to go with him to Nan's party. I promised her I'd ask you," she explained.

"But you haven't asked me, have you, baby?" he demanded, his tone cutting. "You'd drown before

52

you'd ask me for a life jacket."

"We both know you'd throw me an anchor," she replied, pushing the swing into restless motion with one sandled foot.

"I'd come in after you like a shot, and you damned well know it." He sighed, and she caught the smell of smoke as it wafted toward her in the darkness. "I didn't mean to go for your throat this afternoon, Tish. What I said was in the nature of a warning, not a declaration of war. You're only going to be here for two months. I want it to be as pleasant for you as I can make it."

It was an apology. At least, she corrected herself, it was the closest he'd ever come to one. He accused her of being proud, but he wrote the book on pride.

"For what it's worth, Russell," she said quietly, "I don't know how to seduce a man. And I really wasn't flirting. I...I thought I was teasing, like I used to when I was a little girl, remember? It was that...last summer, too, I didn't..."

"Are you that naive, Tish?" he asked suddenly, solemnly. "Two years at a northern college, dating all kinds of men..."

"I never dated anyone," whe replied, "except Frank. I know...what men expect from women these days, and I can't...I won't...Frank doesn't ask..." her voice trailed away to a whisper of embarrassement.

"Are you trying, in your stumbling way, to tell me that you're still a virgin?" Russel asked softly.

"That's none of your business," she returned, her voice sharp because of the embarrassment she felt.

"It's more my business than you'll ever know," he replied, his voice deep and slow and quite in the darkness. The settee creaked softly as he shifted his weight. "Has he made love to you?"

"If you're going to get insulting, I'm going in," she said, and started to rise.

"Insulting?" His tone was incredulous. "My God, did I put that saintly streak in you? If I did, I beg your pardon, I meant to give you a healthy attitude toward sex."

She blushed to her toenails. "Russell...!"

Soft, deep laughter drifted with the muted sounds of crickets and dogs. "Saint Joan," he taunted. "All you need are the robes."

She swallowed, her lips trembling with unreasonable anger. "What did you expect, Russell, that the typical sharecropper's daughter would run true to form and turn up pregnant?"

"Damn you, shut up!" She stiffened at the tone of his voice. It was dangerous; she hadn't heard him like this in a very long time. Tears welled in her eyes and ran silently down her cheeks.

"By God, one day you'll push me too far," he said in a tight voice.

Her eyes closed to blot out the shadowy form so close against the wall. She could hear her own heartbeat, and she was a little girl again, cringing from Russell's fiery temper like a whipped pup.

"Pouting, little girl?" he asked shortly.

Without a word, she got out of the swing and stood up, moving past him slowly, blindly, the tears cold as they trickled down into the corners of her mouth.

She felt his big hand catch her waist, but she didn't look down.

"Tish?" he asked, his voice low and almost tender now, the anger gone.

"W..what?" she choked rebelliously.

His hand abruptly loosed her wrist. Lean, hard finger caught her hips, pulling her unceremoniously down onto his hard thigh. He whipped her against him, one hard arm curving to hold her while the other hand tilted her chin up to his glittery eyes. His merciless fingers traced the tears along her silken cheeks to the soft, proud pout of her mouth.

"Don't you ever," he emphasized softly, deliberately, *"ever* throw that at me again. Do you understand me, Tish?"

She didn't, but it was easier to nod than to risk another attack. She'd never seen him so angry, and she didn't even understand what she'd said that caused it. A sob shook her.

He held her face against his shoulder while he looked down at her. She could barely see his eyes, but she could feel his gaze as if he'd touched her. Against her side, she could feel the thunder of his heartbeat, strong and sure and heavy. His chest rose and fell quickly, and she sat very still, not daring to breathe for an instant. Against her cool face, his big hand was warm and strangely comforting. She could feel his breath against her temple, smell the tobacco and exotic cologne that clung to his body.

Something about the contact made her strangely weak, and almost involuntarily she began to remember that eternity of seconds in the beach-house.

She stiffened, feeling again the anger and fury and pain he'd inflicted on her.

His fingers traced the path of the tears down to her mouth. "You needn't start freezing on me," he said quietly. "I'm not going to hurt you."

"P...please let me up," she whispered.

"Don't be afraid of me," he returned, his voice as soft and sensuous now as it had been harsh earlier. "I used to hold you like this when you were just eight years old, and we'd listen to the hounds baying in the distance and talk about fishing. Remember?"

Her taut muscles began to relax just a little. "You didn't yell at me so much then," she said accusingly.

His lips brushed her forehead. "You didn't prick my temper so often, either. Will you relax, for God's sake, all I can feel are bones!"

"I can't help being thin..."

"Here," he grumbled, shifting her so that her head and breast were resting against his warm, broad chest, her arm caught over his shoulder. "You're still all knees and elbows."

She nuzzled against the soft cotton shirt. This was strangely familiar, the feel and the smell of him, so big and warm and protective in the chill of evening, in the silence of night and darkness. She felt safe with Russell as she'd never felt safe with anyone or anything else. Just to know he was in the house when it was dark and she was alone was always enough to put her to sleep.

"Yo make me feel so safe...." she murmured the words aloud, drowsy as he held her.

Deep laughter echoed under her ear. "If you were a few years older, that would be the least flattering thing you could say to me," he said.

"Why?" she asked innocently.

"Are you going to sleep?" he asked.

"I could. You're so warm, Russell."

"Warm isn't the word for it," he said. His arm drew her gently closer. "Tell me about Tyler and the beach. What did you do?"

"Swam, talked, listened to his mother, played chess, listened to his mother, went shopping, listened..."

"...to his mother," he chuckled. "She looks the type. Possessive?."

"Very. And better than just about anybody, too," she laughed softly, with a heavy sigh. "When she found out I was one of *those* Curries she couldn't do enough to get me together with Frank. That's why I was invited to the coast."

"You were? he asked darkly. "Or your name? Does she know...?"

"No!" she said quickly. "And if you...!"

"Will you shut up?" he asked impatiently. "My God, I didn't bring you home to spend the whole damned two months swapping blows with you."

"Why did you bring me home?" she asked, her eyes fighting the darkness as she looked up at him.

"Was it really just because of Eileen?"

His finger touched her mouth softly, gently. "Maybe I missed you, brat."

"I missed you, too, Russ," she said honestly.

He drew her against him hard and sat just holding her, rocking her in his bruising arms, his face buried in the soft hair at her throat. The sensations that swam through her body puzzled her; vague hungers, restless stirrings made her young blood race through her veins. Her short, sharp nails bit into him as she felt him easing her relentlessly closer to his hard body, closer and closer until she felt his ribs through the muscle as the embrace became no longer gentle or affectionate, but deeply and frankly hungry.

"Tish, are you out here?" Eileen's voice came hurtling onto the sweet, heady silence, shattering it to lovely splinters.

Russell's chest lifted in a harsh sigh as he eased the painful crush of his arms. "We're here, Lena," he called. "What is it?"

She followed the sound of his voice and stopped when she saw the two shadowy forms on the settee. "Gee whiz," she murmured impishly. "Isn't that cute? Russell and his baby..."

"I'll drown you in ice water while you sleep," Tish threatened as she stood up quickly, letting her sense of humor chase away the unfulfilled hungers Russell had stirred. "I'll nail your shoes to the floor. I'll...!" She ran toward the giggling, retreating teenager, and laughter floated back onto the porch as they ran into the house.

CHAPTER THREE

The week before Nan Coleman's party went by in a haze of teas, visiting, and staying out of Russell's way. Tish couldn't explain even to herself why that was so important, but she was suddenly tongue-tied and shy around him. To make it worse, he could bring a scarlet blush to her cheeks just by looking at her, a pastime he seemed to enjoy. Breakfast, for instance, was becoming an ordeal.

"One of the girls I know at school is getting married next month," Eileen remarked one morning over bacon and eggs and fresh, hot biscuits. "She got a job in the office after she graduated, and she's marrying Mr. Jameson. He's the physical science teacher."

"He's a good bit older than your friend, I

suppose," Tish said, her eyes on the yellow mound of moist scrambled eggs on her plate.

"Oh, yes, he's ancient," Eileen said, drawling out the word. "He's twenty-eight."

"Twenty-eight?!" Tish said in mock horror, with a mischievous glance at Russell, who was leaning back in his chair with one eyebrow raised over glittering dark eyes. "My goodness, he's almost ready for the home, then, isn't he?"

Russell's dark eyes dropped to that portion of her anatomy which was visible above the table. He stared with a bold intensity that brought the blood flaming into her cheeks. His eyes caught hers, holding them. There was a new sensuous look about them that thrilled her. "Age has its advantages, baby," he said with a taunting smile. "Although I don't sanction cradle robbing."

"You wouldn't think he was robbing any cradle if you could see them together," Eileen said absently. "Jan is very sophisticated."

"A rare trait in a teenager," Russell commented as he drained his coffee cup.

"Jan's nineteen," Eileen argued, "that's not really teenaged."

"Sophistication depends on the individual, not age," Russell said. He took a long draw from his cigarette as he set the cup back in its saucer and settled back in his chair. He eyed Tish speculatively. "Tish is almost two years older than your friend, but I'll bet my prize Hereford bull that she doesn't even know how to kiss."

Tish's face imitated a beet as two pair of brown eyes studied her as if she were an interesting germ under a microscope.

"Do you, Tish?" Eileen asked, all curiosity.

"Of course I do!" she sputtered, and the look she threw at Russell spoke volumes.

"Oops, I'll be late if I don't hurry!" Eileen cried, looking at her watch. She wiped her mouth with the linen napkin, laying it back down crumpled and laden with coral lipstick. "Bye!"

"Keep it under fifty-five!" Russell called after her, his tone rock hard.

"In a Volkswagen, how could I go that fast?" Eileen called back, "Especially in *my* Volkswagen?!"

"Point taken," he admitted with a chuckle, and Tish couldn't help but smile at the picture of Eileen in her beat-up little yellow bug.

"How did she ever talk you into that car?" Tish had to know.

"Well," he said with a heavy sigh, "it was Friday, and a sale day, and I was trying to load six heifers on the stock trailer...oh, hell, she came up on my blind side, that's all. She was holding my checkbook, and I signed a check, and the next thing I knew I was part owner of a 1965 yellow Volkswagen. At least," he added darkly, "that's what the receipt says. It looks more like a lawnmower with giant tires."

"It's good on gas, I bet," she said.

"So," he replied, "is the school bus. You used to ride it."

"Only because I couldn't get around you like

Eileen can," she reminded him. "I was afraid to push you too hard. I still am," she murmured with downcast eyes.

"I'd never hurt you, honey," he said gently.

"I know."

There was a long silence while he stubbed out the cigarette. He stood up, moving to catch the back of her chair with one big hand while he leaned down, so close that her pulse raced. His breath was on her lips.

"You told Eileen you knew how to kiss," he said in a low deep tone. "Show me."

"No!" she whispered frantically, and her face burned as she met his dark, dancing eyes.

"Afraid, Tish?" he murmured, and his thumb came up to brush sensuously across her lower lip.

"Yes! No! Oh, Russell...!" she groaned irritably.

He laughed softly, drawing back. "Coward," he chided. "I wouldn't have hurt you this time."

Those final two words were the ultimate humiliation, as if he were reminding her of that day last summer, of the angry crush of his hard mouth, the painful bruising of his arms.

"I...I wish you wouldn't make fun of me," she said quietly.

"Is that what I'm doing?" he asked. He tilted her face up to his, and the darkness of his eyes was unnerving. "You're very young, Miss Peacock."

She clutched her napkin as if it were a lifejacket. His nearness was making her tremble, and she'd rather have died than let him see it. "I thought you old people liked having us merry adolescents around," she hedged. "To keep you young, you know."

His big hand slid under the soft weight of her hair to caress the nape of her neck. He eased her mouth precariously just under his, so it was almost but not quite touching. Her heart raced like a drumroll.

"Old, am I?" he taunted softly. His mouth whispered across hers like a warm, smoky wind, teasing her lips.

"R..Russ...?" she whispered breathlessly. Her eyes were misty and stunned and unusually soft as they met his searching gaze.

His hand froze at her neck and tightened for an instant. All at once he let go and pulled his tall frame erect. "Come on down to the Smith branch when you finish," he told her. "I've got a few calves you can pet."

"Calves?"

"Four. All jerseys."

"Oh, Russell, could I?" she asked.

"Sure. I'll have Grover fetch you," he added idly, bending his head to light a cigarette. "Tell him to show you the new App stud, too."

She wondered at the surge of disappointment she felt. She felt...empty all of a sudden, because Russell wasn't going with her to see the calves.

"You used to let me name the little ones," she said, "before I found out about baby beef."

"I used to take you to see them, too," he replied, and his eyes narrowed as he looked down at her. "I

63

can't let you get too close, honey. There's no future in it."

"What?" she asked curiously.

"Forget it. I've got work to do."

She watched him stride away while a pot full of bubbling emotions brewed inside her. For some reason, she wanted to cry.

After the incident at breakfast, Tish was careful to keep upstairs until she heard Russell leave the house, and she did her level best to stay away from the supper table as well. It wasn't hard to find enough old friends, including Nan, to visit in the evenings. And if Russell noticed that her absenses were deliberate, he never let it show. That was the trouble, she thought dejectedly, he never let anything show. It would be good to have Frank for company. There was barely a week left before he and Belle were to arrive, and she was looking forward to it until she remembered how Belle hung onto Russell and visualized her at Curry Hall. It ruined the day for her, even the excitement of baby bulls and thoroughbred Appaloosas.

The day of the homecoming party, she carried the case of beer to the fields without really understanding her own motives, although she convinced herself that it didn't have anything to do with Russell's indifference. In the old days of her childhood, she'd lugged jugs of iced tea out to the rich fields where the harrows had laid the earth open to the eyes of the sun. And she remembered the pleasure on Baker Russell's face, and that of his son, when they drained the gleaming amber liquid while sweat shrouded their sunburned faces. It had been the same when Russell took over the monumental task of overseeing thousands of acres of farmland and the family cattle business. She'd seen him many times with the sweat dripping from his face and arms as he worked from sunup to sundown in the fields. But when Baker sent her away to school, the memories faded, and it had been a long time since she saw men stripped to the waist in the fields struggling with the haying.

Now, sitting quietly in the Mercedes with the sun blazing down on the field hands as the baler spit out bound bales of greenish brown hay, the years seemed to fall away. A twinge of hunger went through her as she looked at the vastness of the landscape and the sweet smell of fresh hay filled her nostrils. In her mind she compared the rustic beauty of this land with the rising steel beams and dirty streets of New York, and wondered absently how she could ever have thought there was a comparison. Russell had called her a country girl, and amazingly enough it may have been the truth even though she'd spent years pretending it wasn't.

As she watched, Russell caught sight of the car and leapt gracefully down from the back of the huge, sideboarded truck where the bales were being tossed. She marveled at his agility, unusual in a man his size. He started toward her, calling something over his shoulder to the denim-clad hands around the truck.

She gazed at him with a new softness in her eyes, tracing the muscular lines of his imposing frame as he drew nearer. His shirt was off, disclosing bronzed flesh over conspicious muscles and a broad chest heavily laden with a wedge of black curling hair that disappeared below his belt buckle. She'd seen him without his shirt all her life...but now it was affecting her in a new and vaguely terrifying way. She couldn't seem to dray her eyes away from him, and with an irritated impatience, she opened the door and got out of the car as he joined her.

He took off his wide-brimmed Stetson and drew his forearm across his beaded, shining brow, and grinned down at her. "If you came out to help," he mused, his dark eyes taking in the wispy fabric of her red and white patterned dress, "you should have worn something more appropriate."

She shook back the waves of her long dark hair and smiled. "Sorry," she told him. "Baker didn't raise me to be a farmer."

He bent his dark head to light a cigarette. "Why did you come?" he asked, and his eyes narrowed as they met hers.

She shrugged. "I brought out a case of beer."

"Beer?" One dark eyebrow went up.

"I know," she said, anticipating the words. "To you, anything less than bourbon whiskey is sacrilege, but it's cold and wet and you look like you could use something. You're soaked."

"The fruit of labor," he said quietly, his eyes steady on hers. "You'll never see Tyler drowning in

66

his own sweat."

"If you're going to start that again," she said, "I'll put the case of beer on the ground and back the car over it a few times."

"Do it, and I'll back the car over *you* a few times," he returned with a chuckle. "Hey Jack!" he called to one of the slender young men who followed the big truck through the field to toss the bales onto it.

"You want me, boss?!" came the reply.

"Lift this cooler of beer out and take it to the boys," Russell told the younger man as he joined them at the car. "We'll take ten minutes. I don't like the looks of these clouds," he added, gesturing toward the growing number of dark clouds drifting overhead.

"Sure thing. Thanks!" he said with a toothy grin. He lifted out the cooler and yelled "beer!" at the top of his lungs as he carried it off into the shade of a lone chinaberry tree past the stopped truck.

A number of throaty cheers followed the announcement, and machinery was left standing in the sun while the men joined the one called Jack in the shade.

Russell laughed deep in his throat as he watched the spurt of energy that the field hands were displaying. "Kids," he chuckled. "Most of them are married with families, but they're just a bunch of boys."

"Something no one would ever accuse you of being, for a fact," she remarked idly. "Didn't you want a beer?"

He looked down at her, his eyes quiet and steady. "I'd rather have had a barefooted little girl with a jug of iced tea."

She looked down at her feet. "If I'd thought of it in time, I'd have brought you some. You look so hot, Russell."

"You've been avoiding me, Tish. Why?"

She brushed at a speck of lint on her spotless dress, trying not to look at the broad chest that her rebellious fingers was longing to touch. "I thought it was the other way around."

"Maybe it was. I've been damned busy."

"I know." She looked up at him, her eyes sketching the hard, sweaty lines of his dark face. "You aren't mad at me about inviting Frank and Belle, are you?"

A cloud drifted over his eyes. "What brought that on?" he asked quietly.

"I don't want you to be mad. I want things to be the way they used to between us," she said, an appeal in her pale eyes that she wasn't even aware of.

"They can't be," he said, his big hand smoothing down the wild strands of loose hair at her back. "You're a long way past your eighth birthday, little girl."

"What's that got to do with it?" She tried to smile. "I'm still your baby, aren't I?"

His chest rose and fell heavily, and the silence between them seemed charged with electricity. His big hand moved, catching roughly in the hair at the nape of her neck to jerk her head back so that he could rake it with his dark, glittering eyes.

"What do you mean by that?" he shot at her.

The punishing strength in those lean fingers frightened her almost as much as his sudden, unreasonable anger.

Her lower lip trembled, her eyes welling with tears, as she looked up at him defiantly.

"You...you great bully!" she choked. "I can't... can't even kid you anymore, you tak everything I say seriously! All right, I won't talk to you at all anymore and see how you like that, Russell Currie!"

"It might be safer," he said flatly. His eyes narrowed even more. "You damned little fool, don't you know the difference between teasing and provocation?"

Her eyes widened like saucers. "Provocation? So now I'm trying to seduce you?!"

The anger seemed to leave him, and a sparkle of amusement danced in his eyes. "I don't think you'd know how," he said softly.

Her teeth clenched at his arrogance. "Frank might not agree with you," she snapped.

"Careful, baby," he warned in a voice that became calm with controlled anger.

"Careful, my eye! Just because you think I'm still eight years old doesn't mean other men do, Russell! I'm grown up. I don't make mudpies or throw rocks...I wish I'd never...oh, you horrible, coldblooded...!" She choked on the words, a sob tearing out of her throat as the tears rolled down her cheeks.

"You damned little fool," Russell said in a strange, tight voice. His calloused hands cupped her face and he bent to put his mouth against her wet eyes, sipping the tears from her closed eyelids in a slow, smoldering intimacy that took her breath away.

"R...Russ?" she whispered, shocked by the action, feeling his heart as it began to pound against the walls of his chest. Her fingers pressed lightly against the thick mesh of hair over those unyielding muscles, feeling the cool dampness with hands that trembled.

"Don't talk," he murmured deeply. His hands tightened on her face, and he drew back to look down at her. The thunder rumbled ominously overhead as the sky began to darken, but the real storm was in his eyes, glittering, furious, dangerous. Oblivious to the sharp jagged blade of lightning that shot down on the horizon like a pitchfork, and the tremor of the very air that followed it, he bent to her trembling mouth. His teeth caught the full lower lip, nipping at it sensuously.

"Open your mouth for me," he growled huskily, his fingers hurting her head, "show me how grown up you are, Tish."

"Russell..." she choked, her breath strangling her, the brushing, nibbling, coaxing pressure of his tormenting mouth making tremors all over her body. "The...storm..."

"It's in me," he murmured against her mouth, "and in you, hungry and sweet and wild. Don't talk.

Kiss me...."

His mouth opened on hers, pressing her lips apart in a burning, hungry silence that winded her. His hands moved down her neck, pressing her body against the whole lean length of his with a frankly arousing expertise, and she never thought of fighting him. Even when his tongue probed at her soft, yielding lips, even when she thought the coiling muscle of his arm was going to break her in two as he forced her body closer.

It was her first taste of a man's passion, and it frightened her. The other kiss had been a punishment, but this was like the end of the world. She raised her arms to his neck just as he stiffened and thrust her away with a glittering contempt that brought tears back into her eyes.

"You were mine when you were eight years old," he said, breathing heavily, "I taught you to ride and hunt and fish and swim. When you were older, I taught you how to handle yourself on dates and how to drive. I'm glad we had those years together. But it's time we started closing doors on the past. I'm hot blooded as all hell, Tish. I can't take that kind of kidding anymore without reacting to it. If you keep pushing me, this is just a sample of what's going to happen between us. I'm older and wiser and a hell of lot more experienced than you are. I took your mouth and you let me. I could take the rest of you just as easily, and don't you ever forget it! Now, get out of here."

Shocked and hurt by his words, she turned and

slammed down into the driver's seat, ignoring his retreating back as she started the car and backed out into the road. He didn't look back even when she turned it and started toward town.

CHAPTER FOUR

Tish walked through the dress shops in a daze, barely seeing the salesladies as she fought a new awareness that caught her breath. Finally, she chose a long white gown that clung like a second skin, its neckline, a low V that just escaped immodesty.

Back at the house, she paced in her room, debating whether or not to go to the party at all. Facing Russell again was an obstacle that she dreaded more by the minute. The memory of their kiss, was still too fresh, and her pulses raced every time she remembered it. Somehing wild and hungry was unleashed in her, something so totally unexpected she could hardly believe she was the same passive young woman who came home a week ago. Her life was changing in a way she couldn't fathom, perhaps changing too fast for her to cope.

"Tish, are you ready?" Eileen called, bursting into the room without knocking.

She paused in the doorway, looking much older

than her seventeen years in the frothy, low-cut blue evening gown that set off her complexion. She glared at Tish's casual red and white sundress.

"You aren't going to wear that, are you?" she asked.

Tish bit her lower lip. "I...I don't know if I'm going, Lena," she said unsteadily.

"But the party's for you! You've got to go!"

A sound in the hall caught her attention. She turned away from Eileen's pleading eyes and looked straight into Russell's dark, unreadable ones.

"You're going," he said, pausing in the doorway, his shirt carelessly unbuttoned, his jeans grass stained, his hair black and damp with sweat.

She straightened proudly. "I'd rather not," she protested.

"If you don't go," he said quietly, "Gus and Eileen don't go. They're riding over with us."

Her eyes fell before his insistent gaze. "I'll get ready," she said in a defeated voice.

"Tish, what's wrong?" Eileen asked gently. "You look so depressed."

"I'm just tired, Lena," she said with a forced smile. "Go on now and let me dress."

The younger girl left with a reassuring smile, but Russell paused in the doorway, his eyes studying her restlessly, searchingly.

"Make it fifteen minutes, honey. We're already late," he said casually.

"All right," she said without looking at him.

"Lost your tongue, hellcat?" he chided deliberately.

She whirled glaring at him with stormy gray eyes.

He only smiled, the challenge sparkling in his bold gaze. "If you were a few years older, Saint Joan," he said darkly, "I'd carry this afternoon's lesson a few steps further. You've got a hell of a lot to learn."

"Don't think I want to learn it from you," she threw back at him. "You're too brutal."

"In that kind of situation, most men are," he said cooly. "I hadn't thought how overwhelming a man's passion might seem to a virgin experiencing it for the first time. You were safe enough. Just don't try it with a younger man."

"I...I don't ever want to try it again," she said, turning away from him.

"You will. Get your clothes on, honey."

She turned around to tell him she could dress without being told when to do it, but he was already gone.

Tish dressed, applied a thin coat of makeup and ran a brush through her long dark hair. She felt very like a lamb going to the slaughter and hated the nervousness that had robbed her of the confidence she used to feel when Frank was with her. If only he were here, she thought miserably, he could protect her. But...from what?

Grabbing a white crocheted shawl from her closet, she curved it over her bare shoulders and went downstairs. Eileen and Russell were waiting for her in the hallway. He was wearing a white suit that accentuated his dark good looks and a rust-colored shirt that clung to his muscular chest like a second skin. As he turned, looking up at her on the staircase, she felt as if a burst of lightning shot through her veins. His eyes traveled the length of her body with a slow, thorough boldness that excited and flattered. They came to rest on her face, and a mocking smile touched his hard mouth.

"Oh, that dress is a dream!" Eileen breathed, wide-eyed. "Where *did* you find it?"

"In town," Tish replied, avoiding Russell's eyes.

The doorbell rang, and, ignoring Joby's efforts to reach it, Eileen went past him like a blue whirlwind, calling, "That's Gus!" over her shoulder.

Russell lit a cigarette, his probing eyes steady on Tish's averted face. "Still sulking, little one?" he asked in a gruff whisper.

"I don't sulk," she replied pertly.

"You didn't fight me," he reminded her with a narrow glance. "At the last, it was the opposite."

Her cheeks filled with color. "Please don't!"

Eileen came back before he could answer her, dragging a tall, lanky redheaded boy by the hand. "Tish, this is Gus!" she said with a beaming smile.

Tish looked up into pale, twinkling eyes. "Glad to meet you, Gus," she said genuinely.

"Same here, Miss Peacock," he grinned. "Eileen's told me a lot about you."

"I understand you're interested in soil conservation," she remarked as they started out the door, and they were at Jace Coleman's front door before the enthusiastic young scholar finished his discussion on soil erosion, sediment control, and the benefits to be gained by putting rock rip-rap on stream beds to prevent erosion.

Nan Coleman laid claim to Russell the minute the four of them went through the door.

"I knew you'd break down and come," Nan said mischievously, openly flirting with Russell.

His eyebrow lifted over a pleasant smile. "Did you?" he asked.

Tish left them there and made her way to the punchbowl, anxious to escape the disturbing sight of her best friend flirting with her...her...what was Russell to her?

The music, provided by a local band, was lilting and loud, and she had to admit that the players were unusually good. They had a repetoire that included pop tunes as well as country-western music, and she was almost immediately drawn into the dance floor in the cleared banquet room.

Between dances, she listened to Jace Coleman, Nan's tall, gray-haired father, while he mourned his crops.

"I can take the loss, of course," Jace admitted grudgingly. "It's just the principle of the thing. Now, it's armyworms!" he exclaimed.

"Buy beetles," Russell advised him humorously, joining them with Nan clinging to his arm. "The country agent says they make mincemeat of armyworms."

Jace set his thin lips. "I started this farm when

county agents were a bad joke, and I'll run it my own way until I'm dead. Then Nan can listen to college boys who've never felt the pull of a mule on the other end of a plow."

"Remember your blood pressure, Dad," Nan teased gently. "It's just been a bad year."

"Tell Russell that," Jace invited. "He planted corn."

"Amen," Russell seconded, raising a glass of bourbon to his lips.

"I haven't seen you take Tish on the dance floor yet," Jace remarked to Russell. "Has this offspring of mine been monopolizing you?"

Nan's full lips pouted at him. "Tish has him all the time. I'm entitled to monopolize him at parties, aren't I, Russ?" she added with a provocative glance at Russell that made Tish's blood run cold.

Russell caught that look in her eyes and ignored Nan. "Do you want to dance?" he asked her.

"My feet are tired," she said quickly. "They've been walked on until they're numb," she added with a nervous laugh in Jace's directon.

"Wasn't my fault," he teased, "I haven't been able to get my bid in for all these young bucks."

"Then, this is a good time," Tish replied, holding out her hand.

Jace shrugged. "They're your feet, Lutecia."

"Not too tired, apparently," Russell chided at her ear as she passed by him.

She avoided his glance and followed Jace onto the dance floor, fighting down a maelstrom of emotions, one of which was blatant jealousy.

Across Jace's lean chest, she saw Nan melt into Russell's hard arms as he drew her onto the dance floor in tune to the seductive melody the band was playing. The older girl's tanned cheek nestled possessively against his chest, and her eyes were closed as if she'd suddenly landed in paradise. Tish turned her eyes back to Jace with a feeling of flatness that lasted the rest of the evening.

Just as the band broke into the slow strains of their last song, she saw Russell walking toward her. Dark and elegant in his suit, he was the picture of masculine sophistication. But under the polish of that elegance, she could feel the raw strength that hours of hard labor in the fields had given him. She could feel the raw power in him that had its own strange magic, that made her so aware of him it was like stroking an open nerve every time he touched her.

"I don't want to dance with you," she protested when he pulled her into his arms and drew her into the dance.

"I know. I can feel it. But I think you owe me one dance, if you can stop being jealous of Nan long enough to relax."

"Jealous?" she burst out, freezing in her tracks.

"Shut up and dance. You're an open book to me, Tish, everything shows in your face." His arm contracted, drawing her closer. "She isn't my mistress, if that's what's eating you."

She stiffened in his warm, strong embrace. "I

don't care how many women you've got. It's got nothing to do with me," she said tightly.

He only laughed. "Loosen up," he murmured against her ear. "I won't accuse you of trying to seduce me."

"I don't know why not, you've been accusing me of it ever since I came home, even though you admit I don't know how," she said irritably.

He laid his cheek against her hair, one big thumb caressing the slender hand he held against his silk shirt. "I could teach you how," he said quietly, and drew her closer. "But it would be a disaster for both of us. I'm thirty-four years old, Tish. You're barely twenty. You need a young man. I'm past the age of accepting limits when I make love to a woman. If you were older...but you're not. It wouldn't work."

"You...you egotistical, bigheaded...!" she burst out at him in a flurry of embarrassed indignation.

"Open your mouth again," he threatened shortly, "and I'll bury mine in it."

Heat washed over her in waves. She lowered her forehead to his chest weakly, hating what he could do to her with words.

"That's better," he said at her ear. "Now listen to me. Don't let what happened this afternoon put a wall between us. You pushed too hard and you saw the consequences. It's over. You'll remember it, and so will I, but it'll teach you not to throw that sweet young body at me."

Her face went scarlet, then it lost its color until it resembled paper. "I hate you, Russell," she said coldly.

"By all means, hate me," he said with a harsh, bitter smile. "It'll be a welcome change from having you hang around my neck like a lovesick teenager!"

He might have slapped her for the look on her face. With a sob, she tore out of his arms.

A shadow passed over his face, and he grimaced. "Tish, my God, I didn't mean that..." he said softly.

But before he could finish the apology—which was as close as he ever came to one—Eileen interrupted them.

"Russ, it's Lisa," she said in a whisper. "Something's wrong. She's on the phone."

He was gone in a flash, and Eileen took a deep breath. "She sounds almost hysterical. I wonder what's wrong."

"Eileen, who is Lisa?" Tish asked, making a grand effort to pull herself together.

She shrugged. "Your guess is as good as mine. She calls Russ pretty often, and he goes to Jacksonvile every month to see her. He never talks about her, and if I try to ask him anything...well, you know how black tempered he can be.

"Tell me about it," she said wearily. "How did you find out about her if he didn't tell you?"

"I overheard him talking to Dad one night after they had had a couple of big drinks. Russ said he loved Lisa and he hated leaving her there." She sighed with a smile. "I thought it was terribly romantic, although you'd think he'd have married her by now. She has the sweetest little-girl voice...Gosh, you won't let on that I told you, will you? He'd have the hide off me!"

A sudden, aching emptiness spread out inside her. He loved Lisa. She was his woman. No wonder he'd never gotten serious about anyone else. Why hadn't he married Lisa? Was she already married? Was she one of those free-thinking liberals who didn't believe in marriage?

"Hey, where have you gone?" Eileen laughed. "Let's go get some punch, Tish. If it's like usual, he'll be on the phone a long, long time. They love to talk."

"Punch? All right," she said vaguely and followed Eileen dazedly to the refreshment table.

Fifteen minutes later, Nan Coleman told them that Russell had to leave suddenly and would be out of town for a few days. She softened the blow with an invitation to spend the night, and Tish, aching from his last attack, accepted it gratefully for herself and Eileen. She couldn't face the big, lonely house that night. It would be too easy to brood over the harsh, angry words he'd thrown at her.

It was a Saturday when Frank and Belle Tyler were flown in at the estate's landing strip, and Russell still hadn't called or come home. Tish went to meet them in the Mercedes, leaving Eileen at her usual place near the stables—and Gus.

Frank moved forward at the sight of her, his blond hair glistening like gold in the sunlight, to lift her high in his thin arms and place an enthusiastic kiss on her smiling mouth.

His dancing eyes looked down into hers. "Food to a starving man," he teased, holding her away to nod approvingly at the revealing pale yellow sundress that clung affectionately to the soft curves of her body.

"I could almost believe you missed me," she laughed. "Hello, Belle, it's good to see you."

"Oh, same here," the blonde said languidly, stretching her voluptuous body in its skin-tight red pantsuit. "So this is life in the raw! My God, it's like the end of the world, Lutecia, how do you bear it?!"

"There are compensations," Tish murmured. "Would your pilot like to come to the house and have something to eat before he starts back?" she asked hospitably.

The middle-aged pilot shook his head. "Thanks, Miss, but I have to be in Atlanta two hours from now and I've got several stops. I'll put the bags in the car."

"It was a nice flight," Frank said with a grin, "but getting here's the best part. I'll need to borrow a car tomorrow, Tish, to check on Bright Meadows."

"I'll run you over," she said evasively, hating to admit that she couldn't turn over any car to him without Russell's permission. Russell! A sharp twinge of pain tore through her mind. Russell and Lisa. Lisa and Russell. She fought the pain and turned back to Frank.

"You're tanner," she teased, looking up at him.

"You're prettier," he grinned. "Gosh, I'm glad you

don't look like what most of us think of as farm girls, no jeans, no dirty hands, no lace-up shoes. I'd hate to see you looking like a backwoods hick."

She bridled but held on to her temper. They were outsiders, she reminded herself. They didn't know the country as she did.

"Where's Russell?" Belle asked suddenly.

"Out of town for a few days," Tish replied tightly.

"Oh, on business?" Belle persisted, her disappointment obvious.

Tish met her eyes levelly. "With a woman," she corrected and had the malicious pleasure of seeing jealousy sweep into the blonde's sapphire-colored eyes.

"Is he engaged?" she asked.

"Not that I know of."

Belle smiled smugly. "That's fine, then," she said, implying that nothing short of a set marriage date would deter her.

Tish led them to the car, and all the way home she wondered which was the real danger, the faceless Lisa or the blond tigress in the back seat of the Mercedes. Either way, she thought miserably, it didn't affect her. After all, she was just a lovesick teenager hanging around Russell's neck on a chain. She'd have given anything to be able to forget those words. As it was, she couldn't forgive him for them.

The Tylers settled in, with cool politeness from Eileen and a strange dampening of spirits in Joby and Mattie. Tish could understand their dislike of Belle, who liked to sleep until noon and have a hot breakfast waiting when she dragged downstairs. But Frank was the perfect houseguest, drinking in the antiques and glassware and elegance of the towering house with an appreciation that lit up his whole face. He couldn't ask enough questions. And he had copies made of some of the fixtures to put in Bright Meadows.

Tish had been with him to the rustic old brick house twice, and she was impressed with the renovation. It was going to be expensive, that was obvious. All the seals had to be replaced, the plumbing and wiring had to be redone. It was a nightmare of a repair job in every respect. But the expense didn't seem to bother Frank at all, he just smiled and nodded at the workmen, a far-away look in his soft eyes.

That Eileen didn't like him was patently obvious. She made excuses so flimsy they fell apart to keep out of his way. Her distaste for both the family's houseguests was conspicious.

"She'd like to have me fried for supper; have you noticed?" Frank asked Tish one day when they were riding in the woods behind Eileen and Gus.

She slowed her gentle mare beside his roan and sighed, watching the younger couple trot along ahead.

"I'll talk to her," she said quietly.

"I hope you will, love," Frank said matter-of-factly. "She's making our visit hell. Poor Belle's just about to blow sky high."

She fought down her inclination to shove him off

the horse and smiled instead. "She isn't used to visitors," she said.

"And that puts me in my place, doesn't it?" he asked with a tight smile.

"Frank, I didn't mean it that way...."

"Of course you did. It's all right, mother does it to me all the time, why shouldn't you?" He raised his head until his nose seemed out of mortal sight. "If you want us to leave, say so."

"Of course I don't want you to leave," she said, exasperated. "I'll talk to Eileen."

"Well, if you insist. Let's ride down to the creek, all right? This is fun!"

She studied him, wondering absently how she could be so unaffected by his astounding good looks and his charm. It would have hurt his pride to know that she felt nothing except a vague irritation. Three days had passed, and she was aware of being both bored and increasingly angry in his company. At the beach, they seemed to have a lot in common. Now there was nothing. And he seemed to be more and more antagonistic. Russell wouldn't like that, she thought nervously.

As she thought of Russell, her eyes softened involuntarily. And as she remembered, the pain came back. There was Lisa, after all.

"Race you to the creek!" Tish called impulsively to Frank.

"Race?" He laughed. "These beasts don't have seat belts, my love, and if I go much faster than this, I'll fall on my embarrassment."

"Sorry. I forgot you haven't done much riding."
She slowed her pace, remembering how quick
Russell always was to take up the challenge—and
beat the reins off her in a fair race, even if she had the
faster mount. His eyes would sparkle with it, and he
was a pleasure to watch when he rode, so much a
part of the horse that no motion he made was ever
awkward or anything less than perfect...

"How's Angela?" she asked brightly and settled
back in the saddle to listen.

It was almost dark when they got back to the
house. They drove up at the front steps, and a
strange sense of forboding made Tish's pulse run
away when she noticed that the den lights were on.
That room was dark, always dark, except when *he*
was home.

"You're shivering, love," Frank remarked as they
went up the steps, and he pulled her gently closer to
his side. "What is it?"

"I forgot my sweater," she lied, pressing against
his thin body for comfort, for support. "I'm just a
little chilly."

She stood back to let him open the door and,
bracing herself, she went through it.

The hallway was brightly lit, but there was no
activity. The den door was open, and with an
audible sigh of relief, she noticed Belle Tyler's back
at the entrance. She was just looking at the room,
Tish thought giddily.

"Oh, there you are!" Belle laughed, turning, and

there was a new brillance in the heavy-lidded blue eyes.

Then, suddenly, Tish saw the reason. Russell moved into view at Belle's side, and she found herself looking up into eyes like polished mahogany. Her heart stopped. He was dressed in a pale brown suit with a cream silk shirt and patterned tie that set off his darkness, a masculine darkness that seemed almost satanic combined with the hard set of his jaw and the black scowl over his eyes when he looked straight at her. There was an unfamiliar flame in his eyes that burned as his gaze swept over her.

She lifted her chin proudly, not forgetting for one instant those painful words he'd thrown at her before he left for Florida. "Welcome home, Russell," she said in a cooly polite voice.

One corner of his mouth went up, but his eyes didn't smile. There were new lines in his face, too.

Belle caught his arm possessively. "I've been telling your brother how much we're enjoying our visit," she told Tish. "I could just stay here forever!"

Tish felt herself burning, but she smiled. "We've enjoyed having you," she said politely.

Belle ignored her. "Russell, you remember my brother, Frank?" she asked.

"I remember," Russell said, and extended his hand to the younger man with an arrogance that wasn't lost on Tish. "How are you, son?"

Frank winced as he shook hands with Russell. "Good to see you again, sir," he said, making a lie of the words even as he spoke them.

"Same here." Russell pulled a cigarette out of his pocket and bent his head to light it, his hair burning with a black sheen under the light of the hall chandelier. "How are your repairs coming along?"

"Slowly," Frank told him. "The contractors have been slowed down on the outside work because of the rain. They're starting to catch up now."

"So Belle told me," he replied, with a wisp of a smile in the blonde's direction. "Where's Eileen?"

Tish's eyebrows went up. She hadn't thought about the young girl until right now.

"She went into town with Gus," Belle said carelessly. "They were going to pick up a saddle."

Russell's eyes jerked up, and they were angry. "I told her that she wasn't to leave this house without permission on a school night," he reminded Tish. "It was your responsibility to see that she didn't.'

"She didn't bother to ask me," Tish returned, locking her jaw for battle. "I have guests, Russell."

"Which is supposed to be an answer?" he shot back.

Tish glared at him. "I can't be everywhere. Frank and I have been riding..."

"Please," Belle broke in with a nervous laugh. "I...I told her to go ahead, I was sure you wouldn't mind. After all, she's seventeen," she added on a gulp when she saw the fury in Russell's dark eyes turned on her.

"Just another teenager, hanging around your neck," Tish said meaningfully, bitterly, and regretted it almost immediately when it brought his furious eyes shooting into hers.

"Careful, baby," he said in a deceptively soft voice. "Remember what happened the last time you pushed too hard?"

She flushed uncomfortably and tore her eyes away.

The front door began to open slowly before she could answer him. A small, black head peeked around it and nervous, wide brown eyes surveyed the small group in the hall.

"Uh, hi!" Eileen called uncertainly, a smile that didn't quite convince on her face. "Has...anyone been looking for me?"

"Get in here," Russell said in the low, soft voice, his fiery temper, bearly leashed.

Eileen swallowed hard and came the rest of the way, her hands folded in front of her as she approached him. "Russ, I can explain...."

"Please do." He lifted the cigarette to his chiseled lips with one eye narrowing dangerously.

"Gus said he was going into town to pick up that saddle Grover ordered," she said in a rush, "and he invited me along. Belle said..."

"Never mind what Belle said," he replied curtly. "You were told not to go out at night when I wasn't home, weren't you, Eileen?"

"But it isn't dark yet."

"It most certainly is."

"Russ, I'm almost eighteen," she wailed.

"So you remind me at every opportunity."

"Will it help if I apologize?"

"Not a hell of a lot." He took another draw from his cigarette. "I'll excuse you this time because of Tish's company, but next time," he added darkly, with a cool, dangerous smile, "I'll have your hide, or Gus's, or both. Do you understand?"

Eileen's eyes glazed with tears. "Yes, Russ."

"All right. Now, come here and say hello properly."

Pouting, she went to him. But he smiled and caught her up in his big arms, planting a brief, affectionate kiss on her lips, and she melted. Wrapping her thin arms around his waist, she let the tears come, and he held her until they stopped.

Tish bit back her own anger at the sight of brother and sister. It was always like that with Russell. He could be cruel when he was crossed, but the anger was always quick to come and go, and was always followed with kindness.

"Oh, Russ, you're such an unholy tyrant," Eileen murmured against his shirt.

He chuckled deeply. "Flattery," he replied, "will get you nowhere."

"I'll vouch for that," Tish murmured, oblivious to the puzzled looks Frank and Belle were exchanging in the aftermath of the argument.

Russell's eyebrows went up as he moved away from Eileen. "Later," he replied, and his eyes narrowed with a threat, "you and I are going to have a talk, Miss Sarcasm."

"Oh, I'll look forward to it," she said with mock

enthusiasm, her eyes spitting at him.

"I know brothers and sisters are supposed to fight," Belle said huskily, "but you two make an art of it, don't you."

"Tish isn't my sister," Russell said flatly, and watched the shock filter into two pairs of blue eyes. "In case she's forgotten to tell you, I will. I brought her here when her father was killed in a farming accident, and I raised her. But for all that, there's no blood between us unless you count a mutual uncle two generations back."

Tish wanted to hit him. It was there in her eyes, in her whole look, although a small part of her was glad that he hadn't told the whole truth.

"Come and get it!" Mattie called suddenly, stepping out into the hall, "or I'll throw it out!"

Forcing herself to laugh, Tish took Frank's arm, tight. "You heard her," she said. "We'd better hurry."

"Would you really throw it out?" Frank asked, puzzled.

"She's been known to," Russell said. "And once, she threw it *at* my father when he made one remark too many about the amount of onions she fried with his steak."

"It was Baker's fault," Tish had to agree. "He and Mattie never have agreed on seasoning."

"Once," Russell corrected as they moved toward the dining room. "The time they conspired to put half a bottle of pepper sauce on your peas when you weren't looking." He chuckled deeply, the sound pleasant and familiar. "God, the look on your face!"

She had to laugh, too, remembering.

"What's pepper sauce?" Belle asked.

"A very, very hot sauce made with hot peppers and vinegar," Eileen told her. "And if you're not used to it, it can burn your tongue up. Poor Tish. She drank water for an hour trying to put out the fire."

"Two hours," she corrected. "But I got even."

"How?" Frank asked.

"I..." She hesitated, wondering how uncouth it would be to tell her straight-laced guests that she'd made a string of Baker's undershorts and tied it to the bumper of his Cadillac for his weekly trip to Atlanta. He hadn't noticed it until the State Patrol pulled him over, and he came home with a face as red as his hunting cap, screaming for blood...

"Go ahead," Russell taunted. "Tell him."

She cleared her throat and avoided Frank's curious eyes. "Later maybe," she said quickly. "Let's eat, I'm starved!"

CHAPTER FIVE

Mattie served them a tempting variety of foods, with country fried steak and homemade rolls, and fresh turnip greens and rutabegas from the garden topping the list. The Tylers seemed to be delighted with the little woman's efforts, and even finicky Belle was complimentary—or maybe, Tish thought maliciously, it was just to impress Russell.

The sultry blonde managed to seat herself in Tish's old place at his side, and she barely took her eyes off him long enough to eat. Tish forced herself to concentrate on Frank's restrained conversation, although her gaze occasionally wandered doggedly to Russell's dark, roughly handsome face. He caught that gaze once and held it with such a raw power that her face flamed and she dropped her eyes to her plate. She hardly looked up for the rest of the meal and barely heard Frank's quiet voice as he attempted to inquire about the color in her cheeks.

Once Eileen ventured a question about Russell's trip, only to have him abruptly change the subject with a hard stare that challenged her to pursue it. He asked Frank about his plans for Bright Meadows, listened to Belle's animated nonsense, and played the perfect host. But there was a static undercurrent that Tish could feel, and when she noticed the drawn muscles in Russell's hard face, she knew that he felt it, too. Oddly, none of the rest appreared to be affected, and that puzzled her.

When they finished eating, they went to the living room for coffee, but in a few minutes Tish excused herself to help Mattie clean up the kitchen. Watching Belle sit beside Russell on the sofa, almost clinging to his muscular frame began to bother her so much that she felt she had to leave.

"You don't need to help me," Mattie fussed, trying to chase her out of the kitchen. "Go talk to your company."

"My company's doing most of the talking," she smiled and went right ahead making the coffee. "Why don't you go home and spend a little time with Randall before he has to go back? He's just down for the weekend, isn't he?"

Mattie's dark eyes sparkled. "Until day after tomorrow," she said. "You know, he's the first one of our family to get past fifth grade except for me. Now he's a doctor, and I'm so proud. Joby and I both are proud."

Tish untied the little black woman's apron with firm hands. "Go home," she said. "While Mindy's gone, it's my kitchen, and I'm throwing you out for the night, okay?"

Mattie laughed and shook her gray head. "I always did think you were impossible, sugar cane. All right, I thank you, and I will go home."

Impulsively, Tish hugged her. "I kind of like you, you know," she teased.

Mattie winked. "I kind of like you, too. Good night."

When she went out the door, Tish started up the dishwasher and was just setting a tray with cups and saucers when Russell walked in the door.

She froze at the counter, fighting down a burning urge to turn and run. Her gray eyes met his dark ones accusingly across the length of the room and everything that had been said between them rushed back into her mind and seemed to separate them like a stone wall.

He stuck his hands in his pockets and leaned back against the doorjamb, just watching her. "Nothing to say, Tish?" he asked. "You were vocal enough in front of witnesses."

"Is there anything that's safe for me to say, Russell?" she asked quietly. "I'm afraid to open my mouth. If I tease, it's provocation. If I touch you, it's attempted seduction. If I hang around you, I'm..."

"I never meant to cut you like that," he said gently. His voice was soft and slow, although there was nothing of apology or humility in his brief statement. "But you started it. It doesn't sit well to have a woman I raised tell me she hates me. It stung. I retaliated."

She dropped her eyes, and deep inside she

97

admitted that he might have had some justification, but it still hurt. "All you do lately is yell at me," she said flatly.

"If you'd open your damned eyes, you'd see why," he growled.

She turned away, puzzled. "How was Lisa, Russell?" she asked curtly, with thinly veiled sarcasm. "Well hidden, I hope?"

She could taste the contempt in the very air around her, and regretted the petty insult even as it left her lips. "That's one subject you don't breach with me, little Miss Piety," he said, his words cold as ice. "It's the one part of my life I share with no one. Is that clear?"

Flushing, embarrassed, she turned her attention to the coffee pot and began to fill the cups with streaming black liquid. Why had she done that, why had she attacked the other woman's existence with such venom? She didn't know the answer herself.

"Who told you about her?" he asked tautly, his voice slicing like a razor in its controlled quietness.

She shook her head. "Something I...overheard. It's none of my business, I'm sorry...."

"You're always sorry," he growled from just behind her. "Not that you made some damned childish remark like that, just that it fired my temper."

She kept her eyes on the steam rising from the full cups, and her fingers touched the tray lightly. "Randall's home," she said, trying to divert him.

"And you sent Mattie home early. Little Saint

Joan, out to save the whole damned world!" he taunted.

Tears pricked at her eyes at the harsh, bitter whip in his deep voice. "Please don't," she whispered unsteadily.

His big hands shot out, catching her roughly around the waist with such deliberate pressure that she flinched. "Don't what?" he growled at her ear. He was so unnervingly close that she could feel his breath on her cheek. "My God, I've fought this until my nerves are raw, do you know that? I saw you sitting there so proud and defiant at the supper table, until you looked up into my eyes, and then I could see the melting start, I could feel the pain. Don't you think I know how much I hurt you? I did it deliberately, I had to...oh God, Tish, I want you the way I want air to breathe...turn around!"

He whipped her up against his hard body as his mouth found hers in one smooth, perfect motion. The hard, smoky warmth of his kiss drugged her and the close contact of their bodies and the strength of the big, powerful arms that held her, caused her senses to swim. He forced her stunned, bruised lips apart with a gruff murmur. His hand, tangling in her long hair, pulled her head back against his shoulder while he tasted her mouth slowly, roughly, hungrily....

"Poison," he whispered against her lips, "damn you, like poison in my bloodstream until I can't breathe! Eyes like November rain, and I see them in my sleep..." He nipped at her mouth, soft, smoky, biting kisses that made her moan in token protest as he tormented her. He drew back to look into her misty eyes. "My God, I could make you give me anything I wanted, and I'm not even trying. Madness, all of it, fourteen years between us and you'll never catch up. No, don't talk," he said when she tried to speak, to ask him what he was saying because her mind was too cloudy to comprehend. "Don't say anything, just stand still and let me taste that sweet, soft mouth. Kiss me, sweet...kiss me."

She obeyed him blindly, her arms reaching up under his jacket and around his waist, her blood surging at the closeness, her breath gasping as it mingled with his, her mouth hurting from his ardor.

The floor seemed to drop out from under her, and she realized suddenly that it had. He was holding her clear off the floor in his hard arms, carrying her.

"W...where?" she managed in a shaky whisper.

"My God, where do you think?" he growled huskily, heading straight for the back stairs.

"No," she protested weakly. "Oh, Russ, no..." just as another voice merged with hers.

"Tish, where are you?" Eileen came in the door laughing, and suddenly froze at the sight that met her widening, unbelieving eyes. Tish's legs felt like rubber as Russell set her back down, and she could only imagine how she looked with her mouth swollen, her hair tangled by Russell's hard fingers, her whole look wild and frightened...

"I...uh...that is..." Eileen stumbled as curiosity turned to puzzled certainty in her round face. "Have you...seen Frank?" she added weakly, with a smile that trembled.

"Where are you, Eileen?" Belle called in a honeyed voice.

"Uh...Grand Central, isn't it?" Eileen cleared her throat and made a beeline for the door, intercepting Belle before she could get to it. "Hi, Belle, she's outside, I'll show you," she said gaily and half dragged the woman away.

"Tish..." Russell began, his deep voice edged with regret.

"It's...it's all right," she whispered, avoiding his dark, steady gaze. "I didn't mean to push you..."

"You didn't do anything. I did," he replied. "Eileen's not blind, little one," he added softly. "I bruised your mouth enough so that it shows, and it was obvious even to a novice that it wasn't one affectionate kiss we were sharing."

"Haven't you shamed me enough?" she whispered shakenly.

"There was nothing shameful in it," he told her, pausing to light a cigarette. "There wouldn't have been anything shameful if I'd made it up those stairs with you, for all that you knew I was taking you to my bedroom. In fact," he said as he lit the cigarette, "that's precisely where I was taking you. But not," he added, meeting her shocked eyes levelly, "for the reason you thought."

"I don't want to know!"

"Why not?"

She flushed, lowering her eyes. "I can't...handle

that kind of relationship, not with any man, but especially not with you. It's too new...Russell, it's...it's...oh, God, you scare me to death!" she whispered tearfully, her emotions raw and uncertain and lacerated. "You make me feel things I never knew I could feel, you..."

"Say it!" he shot at her.

"All right, all right! I can't...I can't...it's comfortable with Frank, it's easy...you burn me alive! I'm afraid of you, Russell!"

"Good God, what is there to be afraid of?" he asked shortly.

But she couldn't answer him. Trembling, burning with frustration and embarrassment, she turned away. Myself, she wanted to tell him. I'm afraid that I'll offer you everything I have, and that you'll take it.

"It's Lisa, isn't it, Tish?" he asked tightly. His voice was deep and slow and harsh in the silence of the spacious kitchen. "You can't cope with it, can you?"

To her shame, she hadn't even thought about his mysterious woman until now. Those burning minutes in his arms had brought a magic that drowned out the world. Now she remembered, and her eyes closed, as she realized miserably what he was telling her; that Lisa was a part of his life he wouldn't give up.

"No, Russell," she said, keeping her eyes on the counter as she went back to pick up the tray. "I'll never be able to cope with it. And you...you wouldn't give her up..."

"No way, honey," he said curtly. "Not even for you. And that says it all, doesn't it? So we'll forget what just happened."

She nodded. Somewhere the sound of laughter came filtering through the walls, but she wanted only to cry. Her mouth hurt from his powerful kisses; her body hurt where it had been bruised against the hardness of his, where his fingers had bit into her waist. But that was nothing compared to the pain in her heart. Rejection was one thing, but to have that...that tramp mean so much to him that he couldn't give her up...to ask her to share him with Lisa...she hated him. Hated him! She turned around to tell him so, but the room was empty.

"Eileen came through the door just as she was wondering what to do about her ravaged appearance.

"I, uh, brought you a comb and lipstick from your purse," the younger girl said, mildly embarrassed. "I didn't think you'd want to go back out there until you...regrouped."

Tish managed a shaky smile as she took the items from the girl's outstretched hand. "Thanks, Lena. Where...where are they?"

"You mean, where's *he* gone. That's anyone's guess," she said, reading the question in Tish's darkened eyes. "He took off down the driveway like a bat out of you-know-where, without a word to any of us. I left our guests in the living room frowning. Better hurry, Frank looks pretty suspicious."

"Suspicious about what?" Tish asked innocently

as she ran the comb through her tangled hair.

"About why you and Russell stayed gone for so long and why Russell came out looking like a madman. Gosh, Tish," she admitted hesitantly, "I didn't know what to do when I walked in...."

Tish managed a smile at that confession. "Thank you for distracting Belle. I think I'd have gone through the floor if it had been her instead of you."

Eileen watched her replace the lipstick on her still-swollen lips. "You know what I'm dying to ask, don't you?"

Tish kept her eyes lowered, but the color came into her cheeks despite her best efforts. "It...it was just a kiss, Lena, and the only time..."

"You don't have to defend yourself to me, Tish," she said gently. "But we both know Russell doesn't play games. He's my brother, and I love him, and I don't think he'd ever do anything to hurt you. But be careful just the same."

"He said we'd forget it," she said, still quietly smoldering when she remembered the cutting words, "because of Lisa. There isn't anything to be careful about. Will you help me carry the coffee out?"

"Sure." She picked up the tray.

"Do I..do I look all right?" Tish asked.

Eileen smiled. "It doesn't show anymore."

"Then let's forge ahead, shall we," she said with a short laugh.

There were dark circles under her eyes the next

morning, and there was a haunted look in their gray depths. She pulled on a pair of jeans and a long-sleeved blue print blouse and ran a comb through her hair. She didn't bother with makeup. Somehow impressing Frank wasn't important any more. And *he*—he'd have gone to the fields by now, she was sure.

But when she got to the dining room, Russell was sitting at the table with Frank, lingering over a cup of coffee. Her heart began to run away just at the sight of him, the pale blue denim shirt straining against the muscles of his chest, his crisp dark hair burning black in the filtered light from the window.

"Oh, there you are," Frank said, rising with a smile as she joined them and looking relieved. "I'm going up to get Belle, if I can roll her out of bed. Russell's taking us all riding. Be back in a minute, sweetheart."

He leaned down and kissed her lightly on the mouth, as if setting his seal of possession on her in front of Russell, and winked as he left. She sat stiffly in her chair, wondering where the devil Eileen was, trying not to be affected by the heat of Russell's intense gaze.

"What the hell was that all about?" he asked curtly. "To remind me that you're his property?"

She swallowed hard. "Where's Eileen?" she asked instead of giving him an answer.

"She left early for school."

"Oh."

Mattie brought in the coffee, and with a murmur

of thanks, she started loading it with sugar and cream.

"You didn't sleep," Russell said quietly.

"I...I slept very well, thanks."

"Look at me, Tish."

She obeyed the deep caress in his voice, her heart skipping a beat when she met the patient darkness in his eyes.

"Why are you afraid of me?" he asked softly.

Her lips trembled, and she dragged her eyes back down to her cup. Infuriatingly, her fingers trembled as she gripped the hot ceramic in her cold hands.

"You're so very young, little one," he said quietly. "A child-woman, like a blossom just beginning to open. I was too rough and far too intimate with you last night. I told you once I wasn't used to limits. All that silky innocence threw me."

She darted a look at him and found a slow, tender smile on his chiseled lips. "I...I was afraid to come down this morning," she admitted hesitantly. "Oh, Russell, what's happening?! I don't want it like this. I don't want to always be fighting you, I want things to be like they used to be when we were best friends..." she said in a burst of emotion.

"Turn the clock back, you mean?" he asked, raising an eyebrow. "After the way we kissed last night, Tish?"

She blushed to the roots of her hair. "You said...we'd forget it," she reminded him with downcast eyes.

"How can I when my blood burns every time I

look at you?" he growled. "I want to tell you about Lisa, I want you to understand...."

"I don't want to hear it!" she cried, jumping up from the table. "Frank!" she called as he came back into the room, "let's go on down to the stables, and Russell and Belle can come later, all right?"

Frank looked from Russell's stony face to Tish's flushed one with a hint of suspicion and more than a hint of jealousy. "All right," he agreed, and let her tug him out the door.

"What, exactly, is your relationship with him?" Frank asked while they waited with their saddled horses for Russell and Belle to join them.

"Russell's like a brother to me," she hedged, her eyes on a car coming up the driveway. "That looks like Nan's Sprite," she murmured.

"A brother, or something more?" Frank persisted. "I don't like the way he looks at you. His eyes look like they could devour you when he knows you're not watching him."

She blushed. "You're imagining things, Frank."

"No, I'm not. If he made you marry him, he'd get all this, wouldn't he?" he asked pointedly, gesturing at the estate.

The shock was in her whole look. "He'd what?" She rebelled at his arrogance, at his attack on Russell. "I'm the outsider here, not Russell," she began shortly. "He told you my father was killed in an accident, but not the whole truth. I'll tell you the rest. My father was a sharecropper, a farmer who works on shares and lives, more often than not, in houses with bare wood floors, leaking roofs, and cracks in the floor! My father had nothing! The clothes I'm wearing right now are worth more than anything he ever owned. If it hadn't been for Russell, I'd be living in an orphanage somewhere, and I'd have nothing!"

Frank's face had gone white, absolutely white. "You...you do inherit, don't you?"

"A share," she said harshly. "The house and land my father worked and probably a small allowance. That's all I agreed to take."

He looked at her with eyes that were suddenly cool. "You might have told me."

"Why?" she asked, raising her eyebrows as she struggled with hurt pride. "Was it the inheritance you thought I'd receive that attracted you, Frank, dear?"

Nan Coleman's little red sports car pulled up at the stables before he could find an answer. She got out, her dark hair unruly, her green eyes sparkling, and joined Tish and Frank.

"Hi, I thought I'd come over and meet your company while I was in the neighborhood," she said with an impish grin. "You must be Frank, I've heard so much about you!"

He shook her hand with a polite smile. "And you're Nan...Coleman, is that right?"

"Nan and her father own the estate next door to you," Tish said deliberately. "That amounts to about a third of the county."

"Russell's got just short of the other two-thirds," Nan laughed. "Frank, you and your sister will have to come for coffee one morning if Tish can spare you."

"We'll be moving into Bright Meadows tomorrow," Frank said stiffly. "And I'm sure my sister and I would be delighted to accept."

Nan looked puzzled, and her green eyes questioned Tish's silently.

"Frank and I are friends," Tish said pointedly. "Right, Frank? Nothing more?"

He straightened. "Exactly," he said formally.

Nan's eyebrows went up, but Tish mounted her horse before she could ask any more questions.

"Come riding with us," Tish said. "Russell will get you a mount if you ask him. I'm going on ahead."

"Thanks," Nan said with a speculative glance at Frank. "I think I will."

Tish turned the spicy little pinto gelding she was riding and started toward the bridle path. As she passed the stable, she noticed that Russell and Belle were still inside. The blonde was standing very close to him, her arms linked around his neck. Even as she watched, Belle went on tiptoe....

Tish put her heels to the pinto's flanks and leaned low over his withers as the wind hit her face like tiny switches.

Tears misted her eyes, and a pain like nothing she'd ever known began to ache deep inside her. Russell, Russell, always Russell, and thinking of him brought a frustrated longing that made her soul mourn. How long, she wondered incredulously, had she been in love with him? Love....

"No!" she whispered huskily. Her eyes closed over the gray anguish that burned in them. "No, it can't be, it can't be! I've lived with him most of my life and I love him, but, oh, God, I can't be *in* love with him...can I?"

But she was. She was deeply, hungrily, mindlessly in love. Suddenly all she could think about was Russell, with his hair burning black in the sunlight, his eyes laughing darkly down at her; Russell holding her in his big arms, teaching her mouth that a kiss was so much more than two pair of lips touching; Russell, who belonged to Lisa, who could never, never belong to her....

With a hard sob, she turned the pinto. She was so blinded by tears that she didn't notice how close to the road the bridle path was. She urged the horse faster, and it jumped the ditch right in front of a speeding pickup truck and the sound of squealing brakes and a horse's piercing cry were the last things she heard as she went down...

CHAPTER SIX

There was an uncomfortable tightness in her chest. She tried to breathe, but even that simple action was almost too much. Vaguely, she felt pain, dull but quite noticeable, all over her body.

Her heavy-lidded eyes opened. A whiteness blurred in them. After a time, a chair came into focus. A small, nervous figure was huddled down in it. She recognized the pale, round face.

"Eileen?" she whispered weakly.

The young girl's head flew up. "Tish!" She jumped out of the chair and hurried to the bedside, resting her hands on the railing. One reached down to catch Tish's and held fast to it. There were tears in the brown eyes.

"Oh, thank God, you're all right," she whispered. "We were so afraid...I've got to call the house," she added. "Baker and Mindy are here."

"Baker came?" she managed. "He shouldn't have, his heart..."

"Wild horses couldn't have kept him away, and he's much better. He and Mindy look years younger," she smiled.

Her eyes searched the room. "Russell?" she asked achingly.

"He hadn't left the hospital since they brought you in, until about an hour ago when Baker made him leave. Tish, do you remember what happened? It looked like the pinto went into the road and a truck hit it."

She nodded. "Didn't...see it," she smiled.

"Russell almost killed Frank Tyler," Eileen said quietly. "Frank kept saying that it was his fault, that he'd hurt your feelings and caused you to run off...he said it one time too many, and Russell planted a fist right in his nose. The Tylers went home yesterday. Frank wanted to come see you, but Russell absolutely forbade it."

"Wasn't...Frank's fault," Tish whispered, grimacing at the pain as she shifted on the pillows. "Why did Russell hit him, *he* doesn't care!"

"Doesn't care!" Eileen's jaw dropped. "Tish, Russell got to you first. God, he went berserk! I've never seen anyone like that. The driver of the truck wasn't even scratched, but it took Frank and Gus to pull Russell off him. Then he got to you and the ambulance attendants had to work around him because he wouldn't let go." Tears misted her eyes at the memory. "All the time we waited while they were working on you in the emergency room, Russell just sat and stared into space and smoked. He never said a word. Not...not one word. And when they told us you were going to be all right, he..." her voice broke. She just shook her head.

It didn't make sense, Tish thought, her mind cloudy with drugs and pain. Russell wouldn't give up Lisa, but he didn't want anyone else to have her...

"I can't..can't think. What's wrong with me?" she

asked Eileen.

"A lot of bruises and a couple of pretty deep cuts, and two broken ribs," Eileen said with a sympathetic smile. "Not to mention a compound fracture of your left leg below the knee. But you're alive, isn't it wonderful?"

"It would be even more wonderful," Tish whispered, "if it didn't hurt so much. I'm so hungry...."

"I'll have a tray sent up. I've got to make some phone calls, but I'll be right back, okay?"

"Okay," Tish said drowsily.

She drifted in and out of sleep after that. When she was awake she remembered Russell's strange behavior. Maybe he felt a sense of guilt; probably that accounted for it. Although at times he did seem to have a genuine affection for her, what he really felt was something he kept stricktly to himself.

"Sweetheart? Are you awake?" came a soft, familiar voice.

She forced her eyes open, and Mindy's small face was there. There were lines of age around the big blue eyes, but she was still the beauty that had overcome Baker's obstinate decision to never marry again when he lost Russell and Eileen's mother. A cloud of silky gray and blonde hair curled around her sweet face.

"Oh, Mindy!" she whimpered and painfully lifted her arms.

Mindy held her gently, careful not to press against

her where the ribs were broken. "My sweet baby, what have you done?" she whispered piteously.

"Acted like a damned Currie, that's what," Baker Currie teased, and she looked past Mindy into Russell's dark eyes, but in an older, harder face framed by silver hair.

"Hello, Baker," she managed with a smile, and Mindy moved aside to let him bend down and kiss the young girl's pale cheek.

"You gave us a start, you know," Baker said lightly, but there was concern in his whole look. "Your doctor says you're damned lucky to be alive."

"I feel like I've been beat," she laughed drowsily.

"No doubt." He ruffled her hair with a big, leathery hand. "Russell's still asleep. I damned near had to throw a punch at him to get him out of here. And when that Tyler boy called and asked how you were, I had to cover Mindy's ears! What the hell is going on?"

"Frank and his sister Belle stayed with us for a few days. You remember, I told you about it," she said. "Frank and I had a...misunderstanding at the stables while we were waiting for Belle and Russell to untangle themselves and come out of the barn," she added bitterly.

"You're losing me, girl," Baker sighed. "Russell's got himself mixed up with a woman? He swore he'd never do that, because of Lisa...."

"People change, Baker," she said tightly. "Gosh, I hurt," she whispered. "Baker, I'm sorry, I'm going to have to stop fighting the drugs...it hurts so!"

"All right, girl, you rest. But when you're better," Baker said quietly, "I'm going to want some answers. From you or my son, or both of you."

She drifted off to sleep on that unpleasant warning.

Drifting, floating, she moved toward a blackness without light or color. She felt a far-away rainbow sparkle through the darkness, and when she turned, Russell was standing there, tall and frightening. She tried to draw back, but his eyes were like black magnets drawing her closer and closer. And, suddenly, as she neared him, a light seemed to glow softly in his hard face, and he smiled and held out his arms to her....

"Russell!" she whispered, her head tossing on the pillow, her dark hair scattering over its crisp white pillowcase. "Russ...!"

A big, warm hand squeezed hers. It felt strong and comforting. "I'm here, baby. What is it?"

Her eyes opened, drawn by the deep huskiness of that loved voice. Through a sleepy fog, she saw him sitting on the edge of a chair next to her bed. She wet her dry lips and slowly, Russell's drawn, hard face came into focus. New lines were cut into it by worry.

"It was...so dark," she explained earnestly, "and I couldn't get to you."

"I'm here, now," he said, his eyes haunted and almost black with emotion.

She sighed, grimacing as the movement intensified the pain in her ribs. "Hurts," she whispered.

"I know." Russell's deep voice was thick with a different kind of pain. "What caused you to ride off like that? Seeing Nan Coleman making a play for your boyfriend, or seeing Belle with me in the barn?"

She felt the tension in the very air as he waited for her to answer the question.

"I...got something in my eye," she whispered evasively, "and Pepper went into the road...Russell, what about Pepper?"

"The impact broke several bones," he said gently. "I didn't have any choice, Tish. Answer the question."

"Why won't you let Frank come to see me?" she replied instead.

His lips made a tight line. His eyes narrowed. "He told me, by God, even if you won't. You told him the truth, and he couldn't take it. He started backing away. If it's any consolation, he's on his knees."

"From what, guilt or a broken nose?" she asked with a dry smile.

He looked vaguely uncomfortable and let his eyes move to the window. "He asked for it."

She held his hard fingers tightly. "Don't growl. It wasn't anybody's fault. Are you still my best friend?" she asked with a gentle smile, not knowing that her whole heart was in the eyes she turned up to his.

He met that searching gaze with a look that might have melted stone. "Is that what you want?" he asked in a deep, soft whisper. "Is that how you want it to be between us?"

116

"There...there's Lisa," she murmured weakly and turned her eyes away.

"God, yes, and you'll never get over that, will you, little saint?" he flashed with narrowed eyes. He stood up. "I'll be back later."

"Oh, don't," she pleaded, "please don't! Russ...!"

He drew a sharp, harsh breath. His face might have been carved from rock for the expression in it. "I'll let Tyler come. That should put the color back in your cheeks."

"Don't be mad, don't go away mad, please, Russ," she whispered through the tears.

"Don't try me too far, Lutecia," he said in a voice that was barely audible. "You can't have it both ways."

One lone tear passed her eyelids. "Russ..."

"Oh, God, you tear me apart when you cry!" he whispered angrily, bending down to kiss away the tear, tracing it back to her eyes. His mouth was warm and slow and gentle on her closed eyelids. "I'm not mad, honey, now hush. Hush."

Her pouting mouth trembled as she looked up at him accusingly. "You big bully," she whispered. "I don't want to fight with you."

"No," he agreed narrowly, "you don't. You just want to wipe out the past year and start over. All right, Tish, we might as well. God knows there's no future for us in any other direction. What can I bring you besides Tyler?"

That hurt, but she wouldn't let it show. "You're really going to let him come?"

"If you want him. Do you?"

She nodded.

"All right." Nothing showed in his face although she scanned it with all her might. "I'll be back later."

She watched him walk away, tall and straight and outrageously attractive.

"You should have watched a few seconds longer," he said as he started out the door. "I pushed her away."

"You mean she..." she couldn't stop herself from asking.

"You know me well enough to answer that. I don't like forward women worth a damn." His dark eyes sent chills down her spine as they gave her body under the sheets a long, bold scrutiny. "Has it ever occurred to you," he asked quietly, "that 'friends' don't normally feel this kind of jealousy toward each other?"

With those pulse-spinning words and a half smile, he went out the door.

When Frank came to see her, she tried not to notice the disturbing reddish blue color of his nose or the band-aid across it.

"I...uh, ran into your...Russell, that is," Frank said with a sheepish look. "Tish, I acted like a damned fool, and I'm sorry. Of course it wasn't your money that attracted me. I wanted you to know that, and know how sorry I am."

"It's all right," she said gently.

"Can I visit you from time to time, and can we still be friends?" he asked quietly. She saw that his eyes

118

were kind but that there was no deep emotion in them, and she was vaguely glad.

"Of course we can," she said with a smile.

He smiled back and bent down to touch his mouth to hers. Just then the door opened and Russell walked in.

"Uh, hello, Mr. Currie," Frank said tightly. Apprehension was in every line of his thin body.

"Don't let me disturb you," Russell replied impassively. "Tish, Dr. Wallace says you can come home tomorrow. Baker and Mindy will fetch you."

"Not you?" she asked involuntarily.

"I'm going to Jacksonville....to Lisa," he said deliberately, and she could feel her face going white. "To bring her home," he added with eyes that challenged her to say one single word.

Her jaw set, her teeth ground together, but she kept her tongue. "Have a good trip," she said quietly, the coolness of her tone at war with the hurt anguish in her darkening eyes.

"I'll see you when I get back," he told her.

"I wouldn't count on it," she shot back. "I doubt if I'll be here."

His eyes narrowed dangerously. "Are you that damned petty?"

"Petty?" she replied. "I think it's pretty petty of you to expect the rest of us to live under the same roof with her!"

His eyes seemed to explode in brown flames. "Better her than you, baby," he said with a cold smile and walked away.

She shook her controlled fury, tears burning her eyes, her heart breaking, breaking...

"Tish, I'm sorry," Frank said gently. "Really sorry."

"Oh, Frank, so am I," she whispered through the tears.

"He'll be back tonight, you know," Baker said the next afternoon, when he figured she'd had the sanctuary of her room at home long enough. "And before he gets here, I want to know what's going on between you and my son, Lutecia Peacock."

Her cheeks were suddenly unusually pink, like the inside of a sea shell. "Nothing's going on. We just argue a little more than we used to," she said.

"Don't hand me that," Baker returned with narrowed eyes. "Russell's lost his temper so much since I've been home, I forget that he used to control it. He walks around with a sore head, and every time I ask him a question he turns red and starts cussing. Is it because of that Tyler boy? Has my son suddenly opened his eyes and noticed that you've grown into a very attractive young woman, Tish?"

"Russell never lets anyone know how he feels; you know that," she said, toying with the wide edge of the pretty yellow-flowered sheet.

"Does he know that you're in love with him?" he asked quietly.

She gasped. "I'm...I'm not! Baker, he's always been like...like a brother to me!"

He shook his head. "That damned Peacock

pride," he grumbled. "You'd die before you'd admit it, wouldn't you?"

"There's nothing to admit."

"The hell there isn't. Eileen told me," he said flatly.

Her eyes came up, and her cheeks burned. "Oh, how could she?" she wailed.

"Because it's something I've prayed for all these years," he said softly, "and now that you've been away from him long enough to let him see that you've grown up..."

"Oh, he knows," she said shortly. "But if he feels anything, it's only physical. And right now, he feels sorry for me because I got hurt and he thinks it's because I saw him in the barn with Belle Tyler. Anyway," she added sharply, "there's Lisa, remember?"

"What does she have to do with anything between you and Russell?" he asked, both eyebrows raised.

"Everything! I won't share him with a...with a...one of those women!" she finished impotently, gesturing wildly.

Understanding flooded Baker's eyes, and, amazingly, he began to smile. "Who told you about her?" he asked absently.

She shrugged. "Eileen overheard Russell talking to you one night about how much he loved her and all. Eileen thought it was wildly romantic. Why won't he marry her?"

"Sweetheart, I think I'll wait and let you see for yourself. Maybe it'll teach you a lesson about jumping to conclusions," he said mysteriously.

"Baker, I wish I knew what you were talking about," she told him."

"Wait until they get home."

"You...you don't mind her coming here?" she asked.

He shook his head. "I love her, too," he said gently.

She turned her face toward the window, more puzzled than ever. "Why...why *is* he bringing her home?"

"Because her aunt's getting married and there won't be anyone to look after her, and that's all the information you're getting out of me." He stood up and left her with a smile and a wink.

Tish was really and truly puzzled by Baker's parting remark, and it dawned on her that something must be wrong with the woman. Blind, perhaps, or unable to walk. And she went through new tortures, thinking about how it would be to have to watch Russell walk with her and hold her, seeing him with love in his dark eyes. She wanted to cry.

The waiting was the worst part. She watched the portable color television without really seeing any of the programs. She tried listening to the radio, and that was worse. She couldn't read because her mind was wandering. Eileen came in to talk, but all she did was make vague replies to the teenager's remarks.

"Tish, you aren't even listening to me!" Eileen said finally.

"I know," she sighed miserably.

"What's wrong? Is it Lisa?" she asked quietly.

Tish nodded.

"I wish there were something I could say. You aren't mad at me for telling Baker, are you? He's awful when he wants to know something. In that, my father and my brother are a lot alike."

She smiled uneasily. "I know that, too."

There were voices in the hall suddenly, and Russell's was one of them. Tish froze, stiffened; her eyes looked wild and trapped.

"It's all right," Eileen said comfortingly. "I'll go out and stall them and give you a minute to get yourself together, okay?"

All she could do was nod, her heart threatening to burst as her dilated eyes locked on the door as if she expected a vampire to come through it.

The seconds ticked away like hours until the voices faded and the door opened. Russell came in leaving the door ajar. His hands were in his pockets as he studied the slender form under the covers with a brief, careless scrutiny. His face had the look of a stone carving, and there was only contempt in his narrowed eyes.

She remembered the last words between them, the anger, the hurt. "Better her than you," he'd said, and now the time had come, and there was an ache inside her that had nothing to do with broken ribs.

"Hello," she said quietly, hesitantly. All the fight

was gone out of her, and she only wanted to run. But there was no place to go, and the resignation was in her eyes.

"Hello," he returned cooly. "Are you better?"

"A little."

"I want you to meet her," he said deliberately. He turned. "Lisa, come in here, honey."

Tish steeled herself for some sophisticated, ultrafeminine siren on the order of Belle Tyler. She didn't want to see the woman whose affection would soften Russell's face, as it was softening now as he looked out the door. The door opened a little more, and Lisa walked in.

She was very small, a little china doll with long, dark hair that curled down to her waist, and a peachy complexion, and eyes that were big and frightened and very brown. And she couldn't have been more than eight years old. A child! And she was the image of Russell....

Tish felt tears prick at her eyes. Tears of shame, of self-contempt; it was all she could do to dam them.

"My daughter," Russell said quietly, his big hand ruffling the soft waves of her hair, an affection in his face that made him seem younger, less formidable. "Her name is Lisa Marie."

"Hello, Lisa Marie," Tish said in a voice husky with emotion and with a tentative smile. "You look very like your Papa."

Russell's eyes speared her face with an intensity she tried not to see, a black scowl bringing his heavy brows together. "You knew, of course?" he asked.

And what could she do except nod? Admitting the truth would have been a dead giveaway. She might as well have shouted from the roof that she loved him, that she'd been unbearably jealous of what she thought was another woman.

"Of course," she said, in a strangled whisper, and her eyes never left Lisa. "Do you like horses?" she asked her.

Lisa Marie smiled shyly, her hand clinging to Russell's. "Oh yes! We couldn't have one because we lived in an apartment and we didn't have any hay," she explained seriously. "But Papa says that I can have a pony if I promise to take care of it. Do you like to ride?"

Tish smiled wanly. "Not very much any more, I'm afraid. I...fell off," she said, and her mind blocked out the impact, the terror..."I hurt myself, but I'm better now."

"You aren't going to ride anymore?" Lisa asked.

"You'll ride again," Russell said in a tone that didn't encourage argument. His dark eyes touched her hair, her cheeks, her mouth. "You'll ride with me."

She swallowed hard, her heart racing wildly under the cotton gown. Her eyes met his, held, caressed, and all the angry words fell away, all the years fell away, and she loved him so....

"Your eyes are talking to me, little girl," he said gently, his voice deep and slow.

She blushed, dragging her eyes back to Lisa, who was watching her curiously. "Do you like to fish,

Lisa?" Tish asked.

"Oh, yes," Lisa said, "except I don't like to kill the worms."

"I'll kill them for you," Tish volunteered. "We'll go one day when I get back on my feet. Would you like that?"

Lisa nodded. "Can Papa come too?" she asked, wide-eyed.

"Papa's only going," Russell commented smoothly, "if Tish promises not to talk for two solid hours and scare the fish away."

She looked indignant, sitting up straighter in bed. "I never talk for two solid hours and scare the fish away!"

"The hell you don't," he retorted. "Remember the last time we went and you told me the life story of your friend Lillian who roomed with you at school?"

"I never!" Tish protested. "I only told you about the super Jaguar XKE that her father bought her."

"And about her father's doughnut chain, and her brother who sold electronics equipment for Western Engineering, and..."

"You listened, didn't you?" she flung back, exasperated. "You didn't say, "shut up, Tish," did you?"

He chuckled softly. "God, if you could see yourself," he said gently, "with your eyes like a stormy day and the color burning your cheeks pink...." The smile faded, and there was something quite dangerous in the look he turned on her. "Will you listen to me if I tell you about Lisa?"

"I'd...I'd like very much to hear about her," she managed weakly.

He started to say something else, but the intercom beside the bed buzzed and Tish pressed the 'talk' button.

"Miss Peacock's boudoir," she said in a pretentious voice, and Lisa giggled.

"Chawmed, I'm sure," Eileen husked over the line. "Dahling, pick up the phone, it's your love one, Fascinating Frank from the fahm down the road, dahling."

Lisa giggled again, but Russell's eyes exploded. He turned. "We'll see you later. Lisa, time to go."

"But, Papa..." she protested.

"You heard me."

"Good night, Tish," Lisa called from the doorway.

"Good night, Lisa Marie," she replied, picking up the phone to turn away from the sudden anger and ice in Russell's dark eyes. As Tish put the receiver to her ear, he went out the door behind Lisa, without a word.

CHAPTER SEVEN

Frank came to see her the next day with a bouquet of perfect yellow and white daisy mums that obviously came from the florist. They were lovely and lifted her drooping spirits, but she'd rather have had a sprig of bitter old coffeeweed from Russell than a bower of roses from Frank. Russell hadn't come near her since the night before. She began to wonder if he ever would again. Even Lisa had been conspicuously absent, as if Russell didn't want any contact between them.

Frank left, and she was lying back in a blue depression when Baker came in.

"Is that young scalawag who just left the reason my son's walking around breathing brimstone, young Tish?" Baker asked with a gleam of laughter in his dark eyes. "He gets worse by the day, in case you haven't noticed.

"I've noticed," she said miserably. "All he does lately is blow up like a puff adder at me. But no, Frank isn't the reason. I am. It's what I said about

Lisa...."

"You didn't know," Baker said, pausing by the bed to give her shoulder a rough squeeze. "How could you? Russell doesn't talk about that child, he never does. Tell him, Tish."

She smiled wanly. "I might as well tell him how much I..." She broke off. "I can't, Baker."

"Coward."

"I sure am," she replied. "I'm afraid of him. I always have been, a little. He's so...abrasively masculine, Baker. He makes me churn inside."

One dark eyebrow went up with a corner of Baker's thin mouth. "That's what it's all about," he said. "That's what a woman should feel with a man."

She let her eyes fall to the pretty patterned coverlet. "Even if it weren't for the things I said about Lisa, he still thinks I'm too young. He...he said something about it once," she added, blushing as she remembered exactly when he had said it, that night in the kitchen.

"Fourteen years isn't all much," Baker said quietly. "I'm seventeen years older than Mindy, and it works for us."

She sighed. "Maybe so. Oh, Baker, I feel so bad. Neither one of them have been in today, did you notice?"

"He saw Tyler coming up the stairs with the flowers," Baker told her.

She shrugged. "So?"

"So he went out and gave the hands hell, from what I gather. Grover was in here a few minutes ago in a lather, with his face as red as a ripe melon, and he told me if Russell blamed him for not getting the cattle sprayed for grubs, it wouldn't be his fault." Baker chuckled. "You see, Russell told him last week to finish the haying first, then spray the cattle. Well, this morning Russell wanted to know why the hell he was finding grubs in the hides."

"Did he forget?"

"I'm not through," Baker interrupted. "When he finished raking Grover over the coals, he took one of the Apps out to be loaded, to service that brood mare of Jace Coleman's for root stock. And when Grover started to tie it in the trailer, he noticed that it was the only gelding on the place—Navajo. Although," he added, "I will admit he resembles Currie's Finest a bit."

"A gelding?" Tish asked incredulously. "Russell was going to send a gelding to service a brood mare?"

Baker grinned. "Doesn't sound quite normal, does it?"

"What doesn't sound normal?"

They both stared at the deep, tight voice that came from the doorway. Russell was standing there, unsmiling, his hat pulled low over his head.

"Grover came to see me this morning," Baker volunteered. "He's ready to quit, and it's your fault."

"My fault?" Russell asked.

"Says he's not sure he wants to work for a man who doesn't know the difference between a stud and a gelding," Baker chuckled.

"Well, hell, I haven't got time to look under every horse I own," Russell growled. "If you've got a minute, I want to go over the production records on those cows we're thinking about culling. While we're at it," he added, shoving his hat back over his sweaty hair, "I think I'll call John Matthews about that option they offered us on the Florida herd. I want to see if he's got official vaccination certificates from the state veterinarian. I'm not risking a bout with Bang's."

Tish was frowning in confusion. Baker grinned. "Brucellosis," he reminded her. "Jace Coleman lost a hell of a lot of money because he bought some cows without those vaccination certificates and contaminated his herd."

"Oh," she said intelligently.

"Got the haying done?" Baker asked as he moved toward the door. "If you need some help getting those cattle sprayed..."

"Why bother?" Russell asked with compressed lips. "I thought we'd mash the damned things out by hand."

Baker's eyebrows went up. "On 5,000 head of cattle?" he asked innocently.

"Grover's got so damned much free time to complain about the way I run things," Russell said darkly, "I thought we'd let him do it."

"Now, son..."

"Don't you 'now, son,' me," the younger man growled. He looked past Baker at Tish, who was listening with laughter in every line of her face.

"What the hell are you grinning about?"

"Me?" she asked innocently. "Nothing at all!"

"Lover boy didn't stay long," he commented, his eyes narrowed on the flowers by her bedside.

"Oh, but the fragrance lingers," she said dramatically, her fingers caressing the blossoms. "You didn't even send me a dandelion," she reminded him, with her face lifted haughtily.

"What the hell for?" he demanded. "They just die."

"So do people," she reminded him.

Something flashed in his eyes, and for a fraction of a second she saw how he must have looked when his mother died so many years ago. Without a word, he left the room with Baker at his heels.

Late that afternoon, Mindy came in the room with a single yellow dandelion, a monster of a blossom, in a cut crystal bud vase.

"I don't know what's the matter with Russell," Mindy said on a gentle sigh as she placed the lovely thing by Tish's bedside on the table next to Frank's gaudy bouquet. "He said to give this to you and tell you that sometimes a single dandelion could mean more than a bouquet and that he picked it himself and it was a hard choice because they were all lovely."

Tish tried to laugh, to return the banter, but she couldn't get the words past her throat. Tears rolled down her cheeks. It was the most beautiful flower she'd ever seen.

It had been two days since she'd seen Lisa when

the little girl sneaked into her room one night before bedtime. Fresh from her bath with her hair still a little damp, she came shyly up to the bed.

"Papa keeps telling me I'm not to bother you," she whispered to Tish, "but I want to draw a pony, and I don't know how." She produced a pad and a pencil. "Tish...?"

"I'm not very good at it, you know," Tish whispered back with a smile. "Are you sure you want me to mess up your paper?"

"Please."

"All right. Would you like to sit up here?" she asked, and moved over to let the child under the covers with her. "It goes like this..."

"That's very good," Lisa said when Tish put the finishing touches on the long-maned pony. "I'm going to name my pony Windy, because he goes so fast."

"What does he look like?"

"He's yellow and with a mane and very pretty, like a collie," the little girl said with big, bright dark eyes. "He's a melomino."

"A palomino," Tish laughed.

"Yes, that's it," Lisa agreed. "I wanted an all-colors pony, but Papa said nobody was ever going to ride one of those ponies again, and then he said a bad word. Why can't I have an all-colors pony, Tish?" she asked.

"I...I don't know," Tish said quietly. Could it be that it was because she had been riding a pinto when she got hurt? Could it have affected Russell so much?

"Look, I can draw a rabbit," Lisa said. "Look, Tish!" And she drew a circle with ears and whiskers and giggled.

Watching her, studying that elfin beauty, it suddenly struck Tish that the child had to have had a mother. Russell had to be her father; she was the image of him. But...he'd never been married, she was sure of that. An illegitimate child might be routine for some men, but Russell had too great a sense of responsibility to refuse a marriage to a woman who was bearing a child. She remembered the long-ago rumors, when he was in Vietnam, about a woman he was engaged to.

"So there you are, young lady," Mindy said with a smile as she peeked in the door. "Time for bed. Say good night to Tish."

"Must I, grandmama?" She sighed. "Oh, very well. But you mustn't tell Papa I've been in here, all right, because he doesn't want me to bother Tish, and he'll be mad."

"All right, darling," Mindy laughed. "Come on."

"Good night, Tish, thank you for my pony," Lisa said.

"You're very welcome, sweet," Tish replied, and a wave of affection rushed over her. "Good night."

With a sense of disappointment she watched the little girl follow Mindy into the hall. Why didn't Russell want them together? Remembering her own harsh contempt for the 'woman' named Lisa she suddenly understood.

From then on, Lisa Marie made a habit of visiting

Tish when Papa was out on the farm and just before bedtime. The two of them were conspirators, keeping their friendship a tight secret from Russell. To Tish, it was like being a child again herself, as she gave the little girl all the love she wanted to give to Russell.

At the breakfast table, when Tish was beginning to get around again, Russell casually mentioned that he was taking Lisa fishing that afternoon.

"Care to tag along?" he asked Tish carelessly as he sipped his coffee and smoked a cigarette. "We'll keep close to the road so you won't have to walk far."

Her heart skipped. "I...I'd like that," she murmured.

"You might as well get in one more bit of fishing before you leave."

Her head came up. "Leave?"

One dark eyebrow went up. "You do remember what you told me the day I left to bring Lisa home?" he asked cooly.

She flushed to the roots of her hair as she remembered herself saying, "I won't stay under the same roof with her!" God forgive her, she remembered all too well. How could she tell him?

"Baker, you and Mindy are going back to Miami pretty soon, aren't you?" she asked the older man, who was watching the clash with silent interest.

"We are," Baker said with a smiling glance at Mindy. "This weekend, in fact, although we'll be back at Christmas."

"Then, how are you going to manage to look after

Lisa Marie and the farm with your busiest time coming up?" Tish asked Russell. "Eileen will be in school, and Mattie goes home at six. Sometimes you don't even get in until eight or nine o'clock."

Something in Russell's eyes began to glow, but it might have been the reflection of the chandelier, because nothing showed in his face.

"If you want to go ahead and stay until after Christmas, that's up to you," Russell told her through a haze of exhaled smoke. "It's only a few weeks."

She looked down at her plate. "The dorms are all empty for Thanksgiving right now. It's tomorrow."

"Two turkeys in the refrigerator, but I didn't notice that," Baker teased.

Tish managed a wan smile as she sipped her coffee.

"Do you want to come fishing or not?" Russell asked.

"Tish, please come," Lisa pleaded with eyes that could have melted a far colder heart than Tish's.

She felt herself being carried along. "All right, if you want me to," she said gently.

Lisa beamed. "Can we go dig worms, like you told me you used to do when you and Papa went fishing?"

Tish averted her face from Russell's scowling curiosity.

"Of course we can," she told Lisa. "You'll have to do most of the digging, though. I'm still a little sore."

"I'm a little girl," Lisa said and burst into giggles.

"Listen to that," Tish teased. "Eight years old and already she's a threat to Bob Hope."

"Who?" Lisa asked, wide-eyed.

Tish laughed. "Never mind."

Russell sat back in his chair, watching them as Baker eased himself away from the table and began to recount old fish stories.

The wind was blowing cold when Lisa and Tish went out behind the stables with a bait can and a shovel.

"Be very quiet," Tish cautioned in a loud whisper. "We'll have to sneak up on them."

"Worms can hear?" Lisa whispered back curiously.

Tish shook her head. "No, we have to listen very carefully so we can hear them sneeze. That's how we find them!"

"Oh, you!" Lisa grimaced and swung at her with a small, open hand. "You're as bad as Papa."

"What does he do?" Tish asked.

"Once, when I was little," she said seriously, "he told me I could plant a blue jay feather and it would grow me a baby bird. And I was little, so I believed him."

Tish laughed. It was exactly the kind of thing Russell would love doing. She remembered once, long ago, hearing him tell Eileen much the same thing. She sighed. Her own childhood had been full of teasing and rides on his broad shoulders and baseball games on the front lawn. All that seemed so long ago now. Russell had been father, mother, and brother. To an orphan, he was the whole world. And now... Her eyes clouded. Now, he didn't want anything to do with her at all. He was so remote and cool, he might have been a stranger.

"Why do you look so sad, Tish?" Lisa asked.

"I'm feeling sorry for the poor worms," Tish replied, and looked sadder.

"But, it's all right..."

"No, it isn't," Tish said mournfully. "Their poor families, having to say good-bye forever, and the funeral expenses...!"

"You're breaking my heart," Russell said from the barn door, watching Tish freeze with a shovel full of black dirt under her booted foot in the middle of the worm bed.

"You don't have a heart," she told him smugly. "Any man who sends a woman a dandelion..."

"Woman?" he queiried with an implication that was lost on Lisa.

She flushed and turned her attention back to the bait bed. "Lisa, will you hold the bait can for me?"

"Give me that shovel before you put yourself back in the bed," Russell growled, taking it away to spoon up two huge shovelfuls and drop them into the bucket. The black earth was squirming with pink, thready worms.

"Where's Tyler?" he asked cooly. "I haven't seen him around lately."

"I don't know, but I'll be glad to file a missing person report with the FBI if you can't live without knowing...." she began earnestly.

He glanced at her with an amused light gleaming in his dark eyes. "Brat," he murmured, and made it sound like an endearment.

"The agony of aging," Tish said to Lisa. "When I was your age, I was his baby. Now that I'm grown, I'm his brat. I think I liked it better when I was little."

"Things were easier," Russell said mysteriously. He picked up the bait can. "There's only one thing left for you to be now."

"What's that?" Tish asked innocently.

"My woman."

She blushed to the roots of her hair. Her eyes jerked up to his and froze at the laughter there. "You do love to embarrass me, don't you?" she asked.

"I'd rather do it than eat. You blush beautifully, St. Joan."

"Don't call me that!" she grumbled.

But he only laughed. "Come on, let's go. I can't afford the time, but I'm going to take it."

"If you'd rather," Tish said, tongue-in-cheek, "we could spend a few hours mashing grubs out of the cattle."

His eyes narrowed, glittering down at her. "You're getting into deep water, baby," he said in mock anger.

She lifted the hem of her jeans quickly, and he threw back his head and roared.

On the way to the pond, Russell detoured by the

house Tish grew up in, his eyes curiously watchful as he pulled the jeep up in the front yard and cut the engine.

The house was without paint. It was old, weatherbeaten, and had cracks in the dark gray boards. The front porch sagged, the glassless windows looked black and forbidding. The tin roof was rusted, and the front steps didn't look as if they'd hold a starving cat. Around the side of the house two lilac bushes stood bare. Chinaberry trees ran down the side of the yard, and a pecan tree towered over the roof in back. It was the picture of desolation.

But Tish was seeing it with a coat of yellow brown paint on the walls and a swing on the front porch; with the sound of singing coming out those windows, the memory of a little girl's happy laughter mingling with it. The smell of baking biscuits was filling her nostrils along with the smell of the cascading pink roses in the bush that used to grow along the bank next to the road. And with her eyes closed she could see her tall, fair father and her small, dark mother as they were so long ago.

"Where are we, Papa?" Lisa asked curiously.

"Home," Tish answered for him, and started to get out of the jeep. Russell caught her hand in his warm, strong fingers.

"Are you all right?" he asked with a tenderness in his voice she hadn't heard for a long time.

She nodded and smiled. "The memories weren't all bad. Mama used to sing in the kitchen when she cooked, until the pneumonia. And Papa...Papa...!"

Russell's fingers tightened. "You watched it happen. I found you there in the fields. I took you home. Remember it that way, if you have to remember it at all. He never knew what hit him, Tish," he reminded her quietly. "I swear to you, he never felt the tractor fall on him."

She grasped his hand as if it were a lifeline and bit back the tears. She took a deep breath, and it calmed her. It was as if she'd laid all the ghosts, all the nightmares to rest.

"Papa, can I go look at the house?" Lisa asked. "I won't go in. I just want to see where Tish lived."

"If you promise not to go on the porch," Russell agreed sternly.

"I promise," Lisa told him and let him lift her outside the jeep. She skipped toward the yard.

"Changed your mind about her?" Russell asked shortly.

"Changed my...oh...yes," she faltered. She stared down into her lap. "She's...very like you."

He lit a cigarette, and she smelled the acrid smoke as it drifted past her face. "You now she's illegitimate?"

"I...yes, I knew," she lied. Her eyes went to the little girl, who was humming as she played with a tall weed. "She's such a loving child."

"Like her mother," he murmured quietly.

Something sharp and merciless stabbed into Tish's heart. She didn't want to ask about Lisa's mother: she didn't want to know!

She felt his eyes on her averted face. "You've never asked, not once. Aren't you even curious about her mother?"

She couldn't answer him, but she nodded. She drew a deep breath. "Did you...love her, Russell?" she asked gently.

"Not, was she socially acceptable, or who was she? What a strange question, Miss Peacock," he said. He sighed. "I don't know, Tish. I was young, and my blood ran hot, and I wanted her like hell. I was on my way to war. I didn't know if I'd be coming back. It was spring, and I took a sharecropper's lovely daughter to a square dance, and the car broke down..." His eyes went dark with the memory. "I asked her to marry me before I ever left here, but there wasn't time...Her sister wrote to me several months later. It was a breech birth, and the doctor couldn't get there in time. By the time he did, it was too late for Lisa's mother. I came home and arranged for Lisa's aunt to take care of her in Jacksonville. I've spent the rest of those years trying to live with it. Sometimes," he said harshly, "it gets rough."

"That night when I first came home," she murmured, "and I made that crack about a sharecropper's daughter..."

"And, by God, you didn't know, did you?" he demanded harshly, catching her roughly by the shoulders to stare down at her with eyes so fierce they made her blanche.

"Please," she whispered, "it...hurts!"

He drew in a sharp breath and relaxed his hold quickly. "God, I didn't mean to do that," he said deeply. "You have a strange effect on me lately, Saint Joan. I wish to God I knew what to do about you."

"What?" she asked incredulously.

He let her go. "Never mind. Lisa Marie! Let's go!"

Tish watched him swing the child back into the jeep with undisguised curiosity. She'd never understand him. Never!

Sitting on the bank of the pond with Russell was like old times, when they used to fish here and she'd talk and he'd get mad and smolder.

While Lisa stood farther along the bank, lifting and lowering her cork, Tish closed her eyes, listening to the pleasant gurgle of the water running toward the spillway. Downstream, she remembered, was a place where the water ran across a dirt road and butterflies skimmed back and forth in summer on the yellow white sand, sometimes pausing on a damp spot to become temporary works of art. Sandflies buzzed there, too, with their vicious bites that left red welts on the skin. And there was always the smell of wildflowers.

"I thought you came here to fish," he chided. He lifted his long, cane pole enough to see that the worm was still dangling from it before he submerged it again with a trail of lead sinkers and a colorful red and white plastic float.

She glanced lazily at him. "I lied. I came here to

remember." But she checked her line all the same. And the worm was gone.

With a groan she pulled it in. "Something out there wants to eat without paying. How come they always get my worms, but they never touch yours?"

He chuckled softly. "You don't hold your mouth right."

She made a face at him and proceeded to dig a worm out of the bait can. "Lisa Marie," she called, "do you need another worm?"

The little girl raised her line. "No, Tish," she called back. "It's still there!"

"Are you warm enough?" she persisted, eyeing the girl's thin sweater.

"Oh yes, Tish, I never get cold!"

"Like her father," Russell murmured with a disapproving glance at Tish's sweater and windbreaker.

"Well, I'm not hotblooded," she said without thinking.

"Aren't you?" he asked in a strange, deep tone.

She kept her eyes on the worm and hoped he wouldn't see the color in her face. "I never realized how horribly cruel this is," she said, hedging, as she threaded the worm onto the barbed hook.

"The taste of fried fish makes up for it," Russell told her with a grin.

"Nothing bothers you, does it?" she asked in all seriousness.

His eyes spared her a quiet glance before they went back to the muddy, deep water. The corks bobbed gaily a few yards away from the raw dirt bank where they sat on upturned minnow cans.

A short, mirthless laugh pressed his lips. "Don't you believe it, baby."

She shrugged, lowering her eyes to the bits of weed and bark at her feet, crushed by her restless shoes. "You're very hard to read. Nothing shows in your face."

"So I've been told. It's damned handy when I'm playing poker. Watch your cork, Tish, I think you're getting a bite."

She watched the colorful float go under the water, bob up, and bounce down again. Unthinking, she jerked on the pole and tore the hook out of the water. The worm was gone. The hook was bare again.

"Tish, did you get one!" Lisa called excitedly.

"Not unless it's invisible," Tish wailed. "Oh, damn," she moaned softly as she sat down and reached for the bait can.

"You're slipping, Saint Joan. That was a curse," Russell chuckled.

"Stick around," she told him, "I've got quite a repetoire when I start."

"I remember. Painfully. You were damned near as hardheaded as I was. It took weeks to break you from profanity alone." He glanced at her with a grin. "But I did."

She grimaced. "Did you ever!...ugh, the taste of that horrible soap!"

His eyes studied her quietly. "This is the way I

146

always remembered you," he told her seriously. "Not in Dior gowns or expensive sandals...but in jeans and old blouses with your hair floating like black silk over your shoulders."

His voice was deep and caressing, and she was afraid to look at him for fear she might break the spell. The soft, deep tone was vaguely seductive; it made her pulse throb, her breath come in soft, sharp gasps.

"Is that why you took me by the old place today?" she asked. "To remind me...."

"To get rid of the ghosts," he corrected. "We did that, didn't we, Tish?"

She nodded. A smile touched her mouth. "We did."

"No more shame?"

She shook her head. "There was something about actually looking at it again, through Lisa's eyes...she didn't think there was anything shameful about it."

"There isn't."

She leaned forward to rinse the dirt off her fingers in the cold lake. "Are you going to keep her here?" she asked, nodding toward the little girl down the bank.

"I don't know, baby. They'll crucify her in school," he said solemnly.

"And you wouldn't step in and take the blows for her, would you, any more than you took them for me." Her eyes met his accusingly.

"I made you fight your own battles, not because I didn't care," he told her, "but because I did. I wouldn't have done you any favors by putting crutches under you, Tish. The day would have come when you'd have had to fight one on your own, and I wouldn't be standing behind you. You make your own security. You can't depend on anyone else for it."

"They'll hurt her," she said, watching the little girl play with her pole.

"Life hurts, honey, didn't you know?"

She drew in a deep breath. "I'm learning."

"Watch your cork. It's moving again," he said.

She jerked on the line too quickly again, and drew out a wet, bare metal hook. She sighed as she reached for the bait can once again.

"I hope I brought enough worms," Russell said carelessly.

"Oh, shut up," she grumbled. She fished out another pink, struggling victim and threaded it onto the hook. "I might as well just stick the worms in the water and drown them by hand!"

Russell chuckled down at her. "They're getting even."

"The fish? What for?" she asked innocently.

"For being talked to death," he said.

Her eyes narrowed, and she glared at him. "You haven't once told me to shut up."

"I don't have to *tell* you," he murmured, and, catching the point of her chin, he brought his mouth down on hers in a brief, hard, bruising kiss. "I can think of other ways," he added, smiling gently as he saw the shock in her pale eyes.

He let go before she could react physically or verbally, and then it was too late. He pulled his hat low over his eyes and tugged gently on his line. "Now, this is how you catch a fish," he began cooly.

They went home with six oversized bream on the mud-stained white fishing line, and Russell had caught all but one of them. The last was Lisa's.

CHAPTER EIGHT

Except for the parade on television and an immense meal prepared by Mattie, Thanksgiving was much like any other day. All too soon, it was over, and Baker and Mindy were on their way back to Florida. Tish wandered around the house with a strange sense of emptiness, of hopelessness. Before many more weeks had passed, she'd be back in college and everything that had happened would be a memory.

A memory, her mind echoed it, reached back to pick up pieces of the past! Russell's dark, quiet face in the doorway of the Tyler beach house; the deep, slow sound of his voice on the porch that first night as he held her so fiercely; the feel of his hard mouth burning against hers as the sun burned against her head in the fields. A long, shuddering sigh left her lungs. The way he'd kissed her in the kitchen that night and stormed out because of what she said about Lisa. If only she'd *known!*

She paused in the doorway of his den, her eyes on the big oak desk he used for record keeping. Despite that brief kiss on the banks of the pond, he was keeping a discreet distance between them. It was almost as though he was afraid to let her come too close. She frowned thoughtfully. Could it be...?

"Tish!" Lisa called from the front door. "Come quick, Papa's going to let me ride a horse!"

"Now?" Tish murmured. "It's almost dark."

"If you're going to come, damn it, come on!" Russell growled at her, looming up like a tall shadow behind his daugther, his irritation showing plainly. "Why she can't move five feet without you to stand and watch is a puzzle to me!"

She felt flayed, not only by the lash of the words, but there was an angry darkness in his eyes that cut her.

"Tish is my friend, Papa," Lisa protested gently, looking up at him with melting brown eyes.

Tish lifted her chin proudly. "I'd just as soon not..." she began.

"What's this about going riding?" Eileen called from the stairs. She came down laughing. "Oh boy, I need a little exercise, can I come, too?"

Russell said a long word under his breath. "Oh, hell, I'll hire a bus and we'll take the field hands too. Come on!"

Eileen grinned at Tish as they started out the door. "Just one big, happy family," she said.

"Blow it out your ears," Tish replied. "I hope his cinch breaks."

"The way Russell rides," Eileen reminded her, "it wouldn't matter much."

Burying a dread of horses she wouldn't let show, Tish sat quietly in the back of the jeep with Eileen, as they bounced roughly over a trail through the fields and along one of the barbed-wire fences that kept the cattle confined to the pasture that seemed to stretch to the horizon.

"Look at the horses!" Lisa breathed, leaning forward to peer through the windshield. "Papa showed them to me before, the Appaloosas!"

Tish smiled at the child's enthusiasm. "Apps," she said voluntarily, "or Appys. Did you know that they're born snow white? It isn't until they lose their first coat that they begin to show their spots."

"That's why they're called the Spotted Breed," Eileen chimed in.

"God save me from back-seat experts who can't even pull a damned cinch strap tight enough to keep the saddle on the horse," Russell growled, his eyes never leaving the narrow field road.

"Just because I once, only once," Tish returned, "let a stubborn little pinto blow out her belly..."

"See the way Tish is stretching her neck, Lisa," Eileen instructed, "if she were a horse that would be called the look of eagles. A horse with a particularly good conformation, with his head held high so that he looks as if he might fly away any minute, is said to have it."

"Eileen..." Tish threatened, dramatically lifting her fist.

"Want some oats, Tish?" Eileen grinned.

Lisa burst out laughing. "You're funny," she giggled.

Tish marveled again at the neat, modern installation that housed Russell's prize Appaloosas and his riding stock. The barns were well insulated and the stalls were roomy and meticulously cleaned. A paddock adjoined each side of the barns and Russell's prized handler lived just a stone's throw away—with the shotgun he kept to discourage midnight visitations.

"This is a big operation," Tish remarked gently.

"And growing every day," Russell told her. He moved toward the corral, outside which three horses where saddled and ready to go—three. Russell, Eileen and Lisa. Tish breathed a sigh of relief. She'd had suspicions....

Lisa made a beeline for the small palomino mare she'd named Windy.

"Lisa Marie," Russell called sharply, "keep your hands off that horse until I tell you!"

The child froze in her tracks and did an abrupt about-face. "Yes, Papa," she replied politely. "Tish, are you coming with us?"

"No," Tish said.

"Yes," Russell said. "Eileen, go ahead with Lisa. But watch her closely. Tish and I will be along."

"Sure, Russ. Come on, Lisa," Eileen called, and quickly marched the little girl to the horses.

"Come back here, you traitor," Tish called after Eileen.

"Bye!" Eileen waved as she and Lisa galloped slowly away.

Tish glared up at Russell. "I won't get on that horse," she said tightly, the memory of the accident flooding into her mind. "I won't, Russell!"

"Yes, you will." That look was in his eyes. She'd

seen it too many times not to recognize it, and it always meant he would get his way. Resistance did nothing but make him more determined.

She looked up at him with pleading eyes. "Don't make me," she whispered anxiously. "Russell, you can't know what it does to me...!"

"There's nothing to be afraid of," he said quietly. "You've got to get back on now, or you never will."

"What does it matter?" she asked. "I won't be doing any riding in the city!"

"You'll be home on vacations," he replied with determination in every line of his face.

"I don't want to!"

He caught her gently by the shoulders. "Tish, have I ever hurt you intentionally?" he asked.

She dropped her eyes to the dusty boots she was wearing. "Yes," she breathed involuntarily.

His hands tightened. "I don't mean...that way," he said tightly, and the memory was suddenly there between them of that summer at the beach house..."I mean have I ever caused you to hurt yourself?" he growled.

She had to shake her head.

"Then trust me. It's for your own good. I won't let anything hurt you, baby. Not ever," he said at her temple, his voice deep and comforting.

She drew a shaky breath, her heart pounding at his nearness. "I can't help being afraid. It hurt so."

His big hand smoothed her long, dark hair. "We'll keep to the bridle path, and I'll be right beside you every inch of the way. All right?"

She swallowed down the fear. "All right."

He tilted her face up to his, and the sudden darkness of his narrow, glittering eyes robbed her of breath. "Don't pick the past up and try to throw it between us again," he cautioned softly. "Keep it light, Tish, or I'll have to come down on you hard. I don't want any more friction between now and Christmas if we can avoid it, for Lisa and Eileen's sakes more than our own. All right?"

Flushing, she pulled away from him. "All right."

He took a deep, harsh breath and turned away from her. "Has Nan called you about that damned party?" he asked suddenly as they walked toward the corral, where one of the stable hands had left a second horse saddled.

"Your birthday party at Jace's?" she asked. "Yes. Eileen and Gus are coming, too."

"I wish to God you girls would clear things with me before you set up parties like this," he said curtly. "It's going to cut me out of going to an auction down near Thomasville. I had my eye on some good farm equipment."

"Do you ever," Tish asked coldly, "think of anything except this farm? We thought you might appreciate having someone care enough to remember your birthday. I don't know why we bothered."

"I can remember my age without any help," he said shortly. "I'll be thirty-five."

"You sound like it's the end of the world. Remember that commercial, you're not getting

156

older, you're getting..." she began.

"Leave it!" The words were like bullets, and the impact hurt, and she stopped speaking immediately.

They were at the horses now, and she looked up at the restless animals with a sense of bitterness. It had been her fault, even if she had been thinking about Russell at the time. But the slow, whispering creak of saddle leather and the smell of horse brought it back. She closed her eyes, and a shudder went through her as she remembered the pain.

"Remember the first time I ever put you up on a horse?" Russell asked softly. "You almost fell off trying to catch the reins? I had to shorten the stirrups two feet to compensate for your lack of height."

She smiled at the memory. Those had been good times, happy times. "You weren't always yelling at me then," she said.

"You grew up, baby," he said in a strange, solemn voice. "Come on, I'll give you a hand up."

She let him boost her into the saddle, and she sat stiffly on the roan gelding with her heart threatening to burst out of her chest. Her lips set in a thin line as she remembered the horse screaming.

"I'm ready when you are," she said quite calmly. Her fingers on the reins were white at the knuckles.

"Relax, honey," he said gently, riding up beside her. "Just relax. I'm right here. Nothing's going to happen."

She let the tension slide out of her with a long, deep sigh.

"Bring your elbows in, that's it," he instructed. "Ride with your knees. He's gentle enough, he won't run away with you. Everything okay?"

Feeling the smooth, easy motion of the horse, the quiet pleasure of Russell's deep voice at her side, the nip in the air, and the wonderful peace of the open country, she smiled. "I'm fine," she said. And she was.

"Russell looks like a thundercloud," Nan whispered to Tish at his birthday party, which, with all Russell's office-holding friends in attendance looked more like a political party. "What's the matter, Tish?"

The younger woman shrugged with a sigh. "He's been like this for days," she murmured. "I think it has something to do with not wanting to be thirty-five. I feel like it's my fault, somehow."

"That he's thirty-five?" Nan asked, and she studied her friend with a curious intensity. "I wonder why it bothers him?"

"How should I know. I see you invited the Tylers," she added brightly. "How's it going with you and Frank?"

"He's all right," Nan said carelessly. "A little too conventional, but nice." She smiled. "Looks like his sister found something to keep her little hands busy."

Sure enough, Belle was standing so close to Russell she might have been a thread on the dark evening clothes he was wearing. Blood surged angrily through Tish's veins and, unreasonably, she wanted to wrap Belle's long black beads around her throat until she turned blue.

"Hi, Tish," Frank said, joining the two women. "It's good to see you. Feeling better?"

"Oh, much," Tish said with a brightness she didn't feel. "I'm the picture of good health."

"You look it too," he said with uncharacteristic boldness, and Tish wondered at the sudden flash of green in Nan's big eyes.

"Thank you, Frank," she said.

"Would you like to dance with me?" he persisted with a grin.

"Only because Fred Astaire isn't here," she replied lightly. "Excuse me, Nan."

"Sure," Nan said quietly.

They moved on to the dance floor and Frank held her close, lifting both her hands to his shoulders in an ultramodern style. "Do you mind?" he asked seriously. "We're friends, and I think the world of you. But Nan..." He sighed heavily. "I guess it shows."

She smiled. "Only to me. Did you have a fight?"

He nodded. "My fault. I always open my mouth and stick my foot in up to the ankle. She won't listen to an apology."

"So you're going to try a little jealousy?"

"If I can make her jealous," he replied, "at least I'll know I've still got a chance. Are you game, Tish?"

She smiled up at him with understanding in her pale eyes. "Nan's my best friend, and she's not happy tonight. I'll help."

He drew her cheek down to his jacket. "Thanks, friend. Here goes."

"Take an old cold tater and wait," Tish murmured.

"Beg pardon?" Frank asked quickly.

"You need a crash course in how to speak Southern," she told him. "Ask Nan when we get through turning her eyes greener."

He laughed. "I'll do that."

It wasn't until the end of their fourth dance together that Nan finally got tired of the back seat and gave in. But before she and Frank got their act together, Tish was already getting the benefit of a furious pair of dark brown eyes from across the room. Russell glared at her openly, contemptuously, from under a scowling brow.

"I didn't rape him, you know," she murmured under her breath as Russell joined her at the punch bowl.

"Of all the damned exhibitions I've ever seen, that one could win a prize. Come with me!" He caught her wrist in a strong, merciless hand and drew her out the door onto the cold front porch. He closed the door behind them with a sharp click and looked down into her wide, misty eyes under the porch light.

"What the hell were you trying to do in there," he demanded coldly, "start the gossips on a field day? By God, don't you ever let a man hold you like that again on a dance floor!"

"But, Russell, everybody does it..." she stammered.

"I don't give a damn what everybody does," he shot back. His eyes were glittering with anger, dark and narrow and dangerous. "I don't want the whole county turning back the pages on you."

"To my dirty past, you mean," she flashed. "You're the one who always wanted me to dig it back up and show the world how poor my people were! Was it so you could demonstrate your own generosity and American nobility by taking a sow's ear and making a silk purse out of it?!"

"Shut up, you little savage," he said in a tone like ice.

The word hurt. It was what the children at school had teased her with when she went to school in flour-sack dresses.

She literally shook with the rage. "Why don't you slap me, Russell?" she choked. "It wouldn't hurt any worse. Thanks for telling me what you think of me. I wish you'd done it twelve years ago...." Her voice broke, and she spun away to jerk the door open.

"Tish...!" he called.

"Go to hell, Russell!" she cried. She ran straight up the stairs and into Nan's shocked arms.

"I can't go home," Tish said when the party was finally over. She was sitting on Nan's bed with a red face, red eyes, and tear stains all over her cheeks. She hadn't moved from the spot all night.

"You know you're welcome to stay," Nan said sympathetically. "It'll be all right in the morning.

You and Russell have always fought like this, but you've always made up, too."

"Not this time," she choked. "Did you tell him what I said? That I wasn't going home tonight?"

"I told him, Tish."

"Well? What did he say?"

Nan looked down at the red patterned skirt she wore. "He didn't say anything."

Tish managed a shaky smile. "As usual, nothing he feels ever shows. If he feels anything." Tears welled in her eyes. "You told Eileen I didn't want her to come up, didn't you? I just...just don't want family."

"There's nobody here but me," Nan said with a quiet smile. "Just your old jealous friend. You stinker, playing a trick like that on me," she laughed. "Frank told me all about it. Finally I had to let go of my pride and admit that I loved him. But it wasn't easy."

"It never is, I guess. Russell really didn't say anything?" Tish asked hesitantly.

"I wish I could figure you and him out," Nan said wearily. "No, Tish, he didn't say anything at all. He just took a shot of Dad's gin."

"Oh."

"What do you mean, oh?" Nan asked. "Don't you know Russell never drinks gin? He hates it; you know that."

She stared at her friend blankly.

Nan sighed wearily. "I'll get you some pajamas, my stupid friend."

Tish bit her lip. "It was his birthday, you know."

"I know."

"I didn't even give him his present. Oh, Nan!" she wailed, burying her face in the pillow.

Nan came back with pajamas and a wet cloth. "Tomorrow it's going to be guns at twenty paces. I refuse to referee you people any more. Honestly, for two grown up adults..."

She went on and on, but Tish wasn't listening. She hurt deep in her soul, and all she wanted to do was cry.

A good night's sleep helped the ache, but it was replaced by honest panic when Nan told her that Russell's big town car was pulling up at the front steps. She couldn't face him, not yet. Oh, she'd have to go home some day, it was inevitable, she'd face it when she had to...but not now!

Hoping to avoid him, she went down the stairs gingerly, her eyes searching the foyer cautiously, but there was nobody there. Not a sound met her ears.

With a sigh of relief, she turned and went through the deserted kitchen, out the back door, and walked out under the huge pecan trees—just in time to see Russell turning the corner of the house. Her heart skipped a beat and then pounded furiously.

Vaguely emnbarrassed, she stood there, her hands folded nervously behind the pair of faded jeans Nan had loaned her. Russell was casually dressed in slacks and a beige knit pullover shirt. He wasn't smiling, but he wasn't angry. She could tell that by his long, measured stride. When he was angry, he moved slowly, deliberately, and his eyes could singe. Now they were dark but calm, as he stopped just in front of her and looked down into her flushed face.

"They want to know when you're coming home," he said without preliminaries.

Tish swallowed nervously. "I...hadn't thought about it," she admitted, her voice subdued. She stared down at the dark brown leather of his dress boots. Beside them, ants were crawling in curvy lines between two small, anthills made of red dirt in the sparse grass. She felt something stick in her throat and knew it was her pride. It was horrible to have to apologize.

"I wanted to call," she murmured, "but I didn't know if you'd even speak to me."

She felt his big hand at her temple, smoothing back the loose strands of dark hair that played in the nippy breeze. "I don't sulk, baby," he reminded her, his voice deep and quiet. "My temper's like flash fire; it comes quick, it goes quick. You know that."

She shook her head, tears threatening. "I only know that it was your brithday, and I...I..." She looked up at him miserably, helplessly, her eyes swimming, her full lips trembling moistly, her cheeks as pink as the inside of a sea shell.

His eyes darkened suddenly, and he looked down at her as if he wanted to grab her and take several bites. The tension was visible in his taut muscles.

"Russ, I'm sorry!" she whispered brokenly. "Don't be mad at me anymore!"

"Oh, God...!" he breathed roughly. He swept her up in his hard arms and crushed her body against his, burying his face in her hair. His fingers bit into her soft flesh cruelly. "God, baby don't ever run out on me like that!"

Tears streamed down her cheeks as she returned the fierce, hungry embrace, feeling as if she'd been half a person all her life until this minute, when she wanted more than anything to stay where she was forever. She might have sprouted wings for the sweetness of the peace she felt. She pressed closer, her arms tight around his neck.

He smelled of cologne and tobacco where her face rested against his cheek, and she could feel the deep, powerful beat of his heart.

"I'm sorry, I'm sorry," she whispered at his ear.

His arms contracted, hurting her, and it was sweet, sweet pain. A hard, deep sigh passed his lips, and he loosened his hold on her, drawing back to look at her.

She met his searching gaze squarely and felt her heart fluttering like a trapped butterfly in her chest.

Russell's eyes went to the long, slender fingers pressed against his soft, warm shirt. "Your hands are trembling, Tish," he murmured deeply, catching her misty gaze.

"I...I'm a little cold," she whispered shakily.

"So am I." His head bent to hers. "Come here, honey."

"R...Russell," she whispered in token protest as his hard, lazy mouth brushed against hers.

"Surely I'm entitled to a birthday kiss," he murmured, "even if I am damned near old enough to be your father."

"Of...of course, and you aren't old, but..."

He nipped at her soft lower lip, his arms bringing her close, safe, in their hard circle. "But what, honey?"

Her hands linked behind his head. "Never mind..." she breathed. "Oh, kiss me...!"

"Oh, good, you're making up!" Nan's sweet voice fell like a bomb on the silence just as Russell's hard mouth touched hers.

"Damn!" Russell said under his breath, and a hard shudder went through him as he let Tish out of his bruising arms.

"Russell!" she whispered accusingly, her eyes bright with emotion as she looked up at him.

"I told you, Tish, didn't I?" Nan beamed, her pleasure at the reunion making her oblivious to the trembling undercurrents of emotion. "Do come in and we'll have coffee."

The tension was still between them when they left Nan's house. Tish could feel it as she climbed into the big black Lincoln beside Russell and leaned her head back against the seat while he put a tape in the deck. The sweet strains of "Remember Me" filled the car, and she wanted to moan out of unfulfilled longing. In the back of her mind she nursed mingled hope and fear that he might stop the car on a long stretch of road and finish what he'd started when

Nan interrupted them.

But the big car kept going, like a missile over the dusty roads, swirling up yellow dust in a cloud behind it, as Russell drove straight toward home. Only a minute after he'd put the tape in, he hit the switch and changed tracks and the heartbeat rhythm of "Forever in Blue Jeans" throbbed through the interior of the car.

"Damn," he muttered huskily, and abruptly pulled the tape out and concentrated on his driving.

Tish watched him, feeling the leashed fury that she couldn't understand, as he lit a cigarette and drew on it, sending clouds of smoke into the space between them.

Another two minutes and he pulled up sharply inside the white and green-trimmed garage and cut the engine. He got out, helped her out, and slammed the door behind her, his muscular arms trapping her against it as they imprisoned her there.

"You're wondering why I didn't stop along the way, aren't you?" he growled harshly. His hands went to her flushed cheeks to hold her face in a vicelike grip while he studied her with blazing eyes. "It's because I'm thirty-five years old, and you're twenty," he told her roughly. "And if that doesn't explain it, I'm not going to."

He dropped a brief, rough kiss on her stunned mouth and strode away, leaving her there with a heavy heart.

The restraint stayed between them in the days that followed. The old times, the good times, were forgotten along with the laughing banter that had characterized their relationship.

Russell kept out of her way with a vengeance, and she went to equal lengths to avoid him. It was noticed by the other members of the family but never discussed. Tish began to look forward to college with a fatalistic pleasure. At least there she wouldn't have to see him every day. And maybe, just maybe, it would quit hurting so much.

It hardly seemed like Mindy and Baker had left when they came back, and the household was caught up in the business of getting ready for Christmas. It put a sparkle in Tish's sad eyes as she and Mindy and Eileen planned Christmas for Lisa.

"What about a saddle for her pony?" Eileen suggested.

"No, she needs some dresses," Mindy said.

"Maybe some stuffed animals," Tish pondered. "And how about her governess? Should we get her anything, since she's only here in the daytime?"

"I guess Miss Asher might like some handkerchiefs," Eileen said. "She likes the frilly ones...."

"I still want a party, regardless of Russell's arguments," Mindy said firmly, tossing her curly blonde head. "The noise can't bother the livestock, they're too far away from the house. Anyway, Tish deserves a going-away party. I don't know how we'd have managed without her."

Tish blushed. "You'd have done fine."

"I don't think so. Make up a list, dear, and let's get

the invitations out this week," Mindy told Tish. "Now, about the tree..."

"Not me," Eileen said quickly. "Not again. I'm not following Russell and Tish through sixteen Christmas-tree lots in the rain so she can veto twenty trees and go back to the first one to buy it."

Tish stiffened. "I do not drag anyone through sixteen..."

"Oh, hell, yes, you do," Russell said as he came through the doorway with Baker. "Every year. But not," he added, "this year. Lisa's going to pick out the tree."

It was worse than being hit. It was as if he was deliberately telling her she had no more place in family tradition.

She got up from the table and hugged Baker on her way out of the kitchen. "You're looking good," she told him with a forced smile. "Feeling okay?"

"Feeling fine." He eyed her mask carefully. "Except that I've got a damned heartless son who doesn't care what his temper hits," he added with a hard glare in Russell's direction.

"Baker, please, it's Christmas," Tish said softly. "I've got to call Nan. I'll see you later."

She went out quickly and headed up the stairs with tears blurring her vision.

"Daddy and I are going to get a tree!" Lisa burst into her room with flying hair, her face flushed with excitement. "Want to come...Tish, what's the matter?" she asked when she saw the darkness in the older girl's eyes.

"Matter?" Tish pulled her mask up and smiled. "Nothing in this world!" She leaned over and kissed the small face. "Nothing at all, precious. Get a nice tree, now, and don't drag Papa over every lot in town before you make up your mind, all right?"

"Is that what you used to do?" Lisa asked as she sat beside Tish on the pretty pattern of the coverlet on the bed.

Tish smiled, remembering. "I sure did. I was a brat," she admitted. "I did it on purpose because I enjoyed being with him so much."

A sound at the door caught her ear, and she turned to see Russell standing there, listening, a look of fathomless intensity in his dark eyes. She averted her face.

"Get going, Lisa, and remember what I told you," Tish said with a smile.

"I will. Bye, Tish."

"Wait for me downstairs, Lisa Marie," Russell said quietly, not taking his eyes from Tish.

"Yes, Papa."

Russell stepped into the room with his hands deep in his pockets, a red turtle-neck sweater emphasizing his darkness. "I never knew," he said softly, "that you did it because you enjoyed my company. That isn't the case these days, is it, Tish? You can't get out of my way fast enough now."

She studied her oval nails with their coat of clear polish. "Even a puppy won't come around if it's whipped enough," she said dejectedly.

There was a long, static silence between them. "Remind me to explain it to you before you leave," he said huskily. "It's simple enough."

"Hatred usually is."

"Is that what you think, little one?" he asked quietly.

She felt herself cringing. It was a kind of anguish to be near him now, to look at him, listen to him.

"Oh, God, I wish Christmas were over," she whispered miserably. "I wish I were back on campus. I wish I'd never come!"

She got up and went to the window, keeping her back to him. "Please go away, Russell," she said steadily, her voice almost trembling.

There was a pause, a hesitation. "Tish..." he said softly.

"Please, just go!" Her voice broke. "Please! All you...do lately...is go out of your way to...to hurt me! Damn you...!"

He took a deep, sharp breath, as if he'd suddenly been hit. For several seconds he didn't move. Then, finally, she heard the door open and close. And the tears poured out of her in a healing flood.

CHAPTER NINE

The tree was lovely. A big, husky Scotch pine with a perfect shape. Russell put it up in the living room and Lisa helped Eileen decorate it. Tish kept her distance, doggedly working in the kitchen with Mattie and Mindy to bake cakes.

"He's hurting, you know," Mindy said mysteriously as they cut out cookies.

"Russell?" Tish paused with her hands dusty from the flour and stared at the older woman.

"Don't tell me you haven't noticed what lengths he'll go to keep away from you. This afternoon was just another ploy. He's so afraid you'll see it," she murmured.

"See what?" Tish burst out.

Mindy smiled. "You'll have to open your eyes, my darling, and see for yourself. It isn't my place to tell you. Let's finish up. We've got to start decorating for the party too."

Tish only nodded. Mindy, she decided was as balmy as the rest of the family seemed to be getting.

Even Baker, was walking around like a cat with feathers sticking out of its mouth.

The presents were opened on Christmas Eve instead of Christmas Day, with all the family gathered around the sparkling, colorful tree in the living room and Christmas music from the stereo filling the air.

Eileen snapped one photo after another with her camera as Lisa excitedly opened her presents.

"Oh, Papa, look!" Lisa breathed as she opened one suspicious box with holes in it and pulled out a snowwhite Persian kitten. "Tish, thank you, thank you!" she exploded, and threw one arm around Tish's neck to hug her while she clutched the kitten gently in the other. "How did you *know?*" she asked delightedly.

"Remember those worms we dug to take fishing?" Tish asked very seriously. "Well, one of them told me."

"Oh, you silly thing," Lisa laughed.

"What are you going to call her?" Tish asked.

"How about Fluffy?" the little girl asked.

"You have to admit, it's highly original," Eileen chimed in, "just the kind of name Tish would have picked."

"I'm going to remember you in my will," Tish threatened.

"Leave me your collection of shrunken heads," Eileen begged. "I've wanted it for such a long time!"

Baker and Mindy laughed at the banter, but

Russell was quiet and withdrawn. A soft light came into his eyes for an instant when he unwrapped the present Tish had given him and found a rare old flintlock pistol to add to his antique firearms collection. He thanked her politely, centering his attention on the gun.

She saved his present to her until last and unwrapped it with nervous hands. She laid aside the tissue paper and found a perfect black opal in a silver setting. It was something she'd wanted for a long time. She took it out and held it in her long fingers and knew that once she put it on, she'd never take it off again. Tears misted her eyes when she realized that he'd known without even being told how much she'd wanted it.

"Thank you, Russell," she murmured.

He spared her a glance. "I'm glad you like it, baby."

She slipped away to her room early, while everyone else was still wrapped up in the excitement of Lisa's enthusiasm at her first family Christmas. She closed the door behind her and pressed the opal to her lips. With reverence, she clasped it around her neck and watched the lights in it dance in her mirror. It was a long time before she slept.

The party was held on New Year's Eve, and it was a less than jubilant occasion for Tish, knowing that she'd leave the next day for college. It would be lonely in the dorm, but maybe her friend Lillian would arrive early too. She tried not to think about it, smoothing her long white gown over her thinness as she joined the throng in the living room.

The music from the stereo was loud, and ice clinked merrily in crystal glasses. Nan was here, and Belle Tyler and, of course, Frank. Russell didn't like that, and he couldn't have been more obvious about it, the way he was ignoring Frank.

Tish sighed into her weak drink, which was mostly water and ice, as she stood by herself against the wall and watched the guests. Things between her and Russell were so strained that it was an effort to be in the same room with him. Although tonight his eyes were on her most of the time. She met them across the room and saw them smoldering, quiet....

She'd rather have been in the kitchen with Mattie, or out on the porch, snuggled in her coat watching the night sky, accompanied only by the lonely sound of the wind. She'd rather have been anywhere, in fact, but here, where she had to watch Belle Tyler clinging to Russell's arm as if it were the only safe harbor in a sea of people.

The noise and confusion grew worse by the minute. That, and Belle, finally bothered her so much that she started easing toward the door to make her escape.

Before she got past the arched doorway, she bumped into something big and warm and solid, and, looking up, she found Russell standing between her and freedom.

"Running out?" he asked with a quiet smile. "They'll be blowing the noisemakers in about..." he looked at the black watch imbedded in the fine hairs on his wrist, "forty more seconds."

"I...that is, the noise," she faltered. "I just wanted to get away from it."

"From the noise, Tish," he asked deliberately, "or from the sight of Tyler's sister wrapping herself around me?"

Her eyes flashed gray fire up at him. "If you think I'm jealous of you...."

But before she could finish the tirade, the unmistakable strains of "Auld Lang Syne" filled the room and everything except Russell's dark face and eyes disappeared. He caught her small waist with two big hands and jerked her against him.

"Be still, Tish," he said when she tried to draw back. "It's the witching hour, and you're going to help me get that blonde off my back. I'm going to kiss you, Miss Peacock," he murmured as he drew her even closer. His breath was warm and whiskey-scented against her forehead, her eyes, as he looked down into her stunned, pink face. "I'm going to taste that soft mouth until I make you tremble in front of God and Belle Tyler and the rest of them."

"Oh, Russell, you musn't," she whispered shakily. The words he was saying made her weak, made her breath rustle in her throat.

"Why not, honey?" he whispered. His big hand tangled in her loosened hair, drawing her head back against his broad shoulder. "We've kissed like this before, remember? That night I came home from Jacksonville we were burning each other alive when

177

Eileen walked in on us...."

"They're...they're staring," she whispered, red faced. Sensation after sensation was washing over her slender body as it rested fully against his.

"Let them stare," he murmured, his voice deep and slow and husky with emotion. "Kiss me, Tish...come into the fire and see how it burns."

His mouth opened on hers. His strong arms drew her against the big, warm body, and she gave herself up to the flames that burned and burned and burned....

He drew back a breath, his eyes fathomless, strange, dark with a hunger that was unmistakable. "Let's go."

"Go...where?" she whispered as he took her arm and led her out of the room into the foyer.

He didn't bother with an answer. Unlocking the door to his den with a key, he opened it and drew her inside, not even pausing to turn on the overhead light as he locked the door behind them.

"What...what will they think, the way we..." Tish faltered unsteadily.

He lifted her completely off the floor in his hard arms and carried her to the soft, white shag rug in front of the fireplace. He laid her down on it gently, almost reverently, and stretched out beside her, pausing just long enough to shed his jacket and his tie and loosen the top buttons of his shirt.

"Don't talk to me, Lutecia," he said in a dark, tight whisper.

"What...what are you..." she protested weakly,

her palms pressed ineffectively against the broad, hard chest above her.

"I brought you in here to say good-bye," he said with self-contempt in every line of his face. "I want the taste of your mouth under mine, the softness of that sweet, young body against me for a few minutes before you walk out of my life," he breathed softly. "My God, can't you see how it is with me...how it's been this whole year? Don't you know that I've damned near had to tie my hands behind me to keep them off you?" He drew a long, harsh breath. "Tonight, I don't care. I want these few minutes with you...just a few minutes out of two lifetimes to say good-bye in a much more satisfactory way than with words...let me show you, baby..." he breathed as his mouth touched hers.

Her hands trembled against his chest as he kissed her slowly, gently, his lips playing with hers in silence. Her heart pounded, ached, at this miracle of feeling that swept over her, the joy of being close, being loved by that hard, skillfull mouth...

"Here," he murmured, drawing her fingers to the buttons of his shirt. "Unfasten it."

She obeyed him hesitantly, her hands fumbling with the stubborn buttons in silence until she had it open halfway down his chest, until she could feel the crisp hair that covered the warm, smooth muscles.

She looked up at him with awe in her whole expression, touching him, feeling the sensuous masculinity at her fingertips as she touched him with them.

His dark eyes searched hers. "Never, Tish?" he asked, his voice caressing as he read the newness of the action in her eyes.

She managed to shake her head, the pounding of her heart making her tongue-tied.

His lips touched her forehead, her eyelids, her nose, her cheeks in a soft, sweet tasting that made ripples of pleasure all the way to her toes. No man had ever been so exquisitely gentle with her.

"I haven't made love like this since I was sixteen," he murmured against her hair.

"But..I mean, isn't this usually..." she tried to put the question into words foggily.

He chuckled tenderly. "If you were any other woman, I'd have half your clothes off by now," he said matter-of-factly.

"Russell Currie!" she gasped.

"Relax," he whispered, amusement making his voice sound like silk. "Just relax. It's not going that far with us. I can't risk it. A few kisses, little saint, that's all I want. It would make vacations here unbearable if we went any further, and you know it."

"Would it?"

He took her face in his big hands and held it while his mouth explored hers in a long, slow, hungry kiss that never seemed to end. The tenderness in it brought tears to her eyes when she opened them and looked up at him.

"Russ," she whispered brokenly, drowning in the anguish of leaving him, of loving him. "Oh, Russ, I love you so much, so very much! I..."

He pressed a long, hard finger against her lips and something in his eyes flashed like brown lightning. "Don't say it," he said tightly. "Not like that!"

"But, I do, I..." she whispered feverishly.

He dragged himself away from her and stood up, pausing to light a cigarette as he stared down into the flames. "I know," he said finally. "I've known for a long time. It's one reason I've kept rippling at your temper, little girl. I told you once before there was no future in it, and I wasn't kidding."

She stared down at the softness of the shag rug, clutching it with her fingers as she felt her pride fall away. "I didn't know about Lisa, if that's why..."

"Good God, I knew that!" he exploded. "I knew it the moment you saw her. Nothing you said could have disguised that look in your eyes. No, Tish, it's not Lisa. Not directly anyway." His eyes swept over her where she lay on the rug, and he tore them away with a muffled curse. "Will you please, for God's sake, sit up?" he growled.

The whip of his voice brought her into a sitting position, snapping at her frayed nerves. "I'm sorry," she murmured. "I...I guess I had too much to drink, I didn't mean to..."

"There are fifteen years between us, damn it!" he said harshly, his eyes narrow and hot and hurting, although she didn't see that with her eyes downcast. "Fifteen years, Tish—a generation. You've been a baby until this year, and you've only grown up because of what I've taught you to feel. But that isn't the kind of love you need from a man; it's not even love, Tish, it's just..."

"Don't," she whispered, sick with embarrassment, humiliation.

He shrugged. "Well," he sighed, "you get the drift, don't you? You're not old enough or sophisticated enough for me, little one. It wouldn't work. The years are wrong."

Added to which, she thought, and the thought was unbearable, you don't love me. You just...want me.

She got to her feet. "I'm sorry if I've embarrassed you," she said with what quiet dignity she could muster, her voice soft with hurt. "It won't ever happen again."

Her eyes misted as she went to the door, knowing that if she forgot everything else, she'd never get over those minutes in his hard arms when her age hadn't seemed to matter to him...

"Tish..." he said in a strained, tight voice.

"It's all right," she managed in a calm voice. "Like you said, it was just...physical. Good night, Russell."

"God in heaven...! Tish!" he called after her.

But she was out the door and running, and she didn't stop until she got to the head of the stairs.

Life in the dorm was chaotic, but Tish shuffled back into the routine with a brittle fervor. And if her eyes looked haunted or her thinness gave away the sleepless nights, her friends put it down to the pressure of hard work.

Lillian wanted to know all about Frank, all about the farm, all about the vacation, and Tish answered her petite blue-eyed roommate with quiet enthusiasm.

Lillian had a new boyfriend who played the bagpipes in a band and worked at a restaurant off campus. It made Tish even lonelier at night when she studied while Lillian was out. Even the friendly banter of the other girls and the nonsense that was constantly being carried on didn't soothe her lacerated feelings.

She could still see Russell the way he'd looked when she left that morning: dark-eyed, quiet, vaguely angry. She hadn't met his eyes. That hadn't been possible. She said the conventional words, ignored Lisa's tears as she hugged the child, and rode away toward the airport in a fog of pain.

Baker, Mindy, and Eileen, seemed to sense that something was very wrong between her and Russell, but they were kind enough not to pump her.

The weeks had passed quickly, despite the killing hunger that hadn't given her a day's peace. Mindy wrote, but her letters conspicuously didn't mention Russell. And when Tish wrote back, she didn't, either. She hadn't given any indication that living without him was like walking around dead, although it felt like it. If only she could forget...!

"There's somebody downstairs," Lillian broke into her thoughts.

"What?" Tish asked, looking up from her English composition book.

"A man," Lillian said excitedly. "And what a man! Tish, you've been holding out on me! If I'd known Frank Tyler was *that* good looking, I'd have gone to the coast with you!"

Frank? Here? With a dejected sigh, Tish closed the book, pulled off her gown and threw on a pair of slacks and a white sweater. She paused to run a brush through her long hair, leaving her face bare of makeup, and went downstairs. She couldn't imagine why Frank would come all this way, unless he was in town on business and just dropped by to...

Her gasp was audible. She was at the foot of the stairs, and he was the only one in the living room. But he wasn't Frank. He was too tall, and his shoulders were too broad, and his hair was too black.

He turned and looked with eyes she could barely meet, so brown and dark and strange that they made her heart run away.

She forced her feet to move and joined him in the spacious living room, stopping several feet away. "Hello, Russell," she said in a tight, polite voice. "How nice to see you."

His eyes studied her wan face and grew narrower by the minute. He looked older, himself. And different, somehow. Lonely...

"Lisa misses you," he said quietly.

"I miss her, too." She swallowed nervously. "Would you like to sit down..."

"Oh, God, Tish," he whispered huskily, "come here!"

His arms caught her roughly, slamming her against his hard body, his head bending to hers, "Tish..."

His mouth opened on hers, hurting, bruising, his arms cruel as he stilled her feeble struggles, his mouth demanding, devouring as he kissed her with a need that made him tremble, made his heart shake her with its heavy beat. A sob broke from her lips at the intensity of emotion that was transferred from him to her as the nature of the fiery kiss changed suddenly, became searching and tender, asking, exploring, seeking answers that she was yielding up tremulously as her mouth betrayed her and told him how lonely the weeks had been, how empty.

He drew back a breath, his eyes dark and sensuous, his hair mussed by her fingers, his mouth firm and hard as it poised over hers.

"Your lips are telling me things you never would," he said huskily. "Miss me?"

She nodded, shaken by the suddenness of it all.

"Little girl, don't you think I know what a damned, pig-headed fool I've been?" he asked quietly. "Do you know how many nights I've lain awake remembering the feel of you in my arms, the taste of tears on your mouth when I kissed you...my God, Tish, do you know that life has been a waking nightmare since I let you walk out that door? I never knew how empty the world could be, how colorless, until I tried to live in it without you."·

Her mind whirled at the emotion in his voice. "But you..."

"Do you remember that night in the kitchen," he whispered, "when I started up the stairs with you? Do you know what I meant to do?"

She blushed. "You said it wasn't the reason I thought."

He pulled a tiny box out of his jacket pocket. "I had this in my chest of drawers," he said deeply. "I was going to give it to you. I bought it in New York last summer on a business trip, just after the incident in the beach house.."

She opened it, and found a perfect ruby surrounded by tiny diamonds—an engagement ring! Her eyes met his and everything she felt was in them.

"I love you like hell on fire, Tish," he whispered as his mouth brushed against hers. "I've been fighting it ever since I held you in my arms in that beach house and felt your mouth tremble under mine. I'm not fighting it any more. We'll get married, And I'll worry about those fifteen years in my spare time..."

"Spare time?" she murmured against his hard mouth.

"In between our first son, and our next daughter..." he breathed. "Pack your bag. I left the Cessna running at the airport."

"I don't need to take anything with me," she said, her eyes bright with love, with paradise at her fingertips. "I've got my world right here."

MacFadden Romances

#**1**		33026	**SWEET DECEPTION** Alice Livingston	$1.25
#**2**		33027	**THE WIDOW AND THE WANDERER** Ellen O'Sullivan	$1.25
#**3**		33017	**FIRST LOVE** Lillian Crawford	$1.25
#**4**		33020	**DAWN OF LOVE** Marie Collinson	$1.25
#**5**		33005	**THE IVORY PRINCESS** Elise Delatour	$1.25
#**6**		33006	**THE WAY OF LOVE** Margary Beauchamp	$1.25
#**8**		33008	**BLUE SKIES, WHITE SANDS** Lucy Merwin	$1.25
#**9**		33009	**THE WINDS OF PARADISE** Grace Caldwell	$1.25
#**10**		33010	**NIGHT OF THE TEMPEST** Elizabeth Callahan	$1.25

☐ Send me a free list of all your books in print.

_____

MacFadden Romances—
A Division of Kim Publishing Corp.
432 Park Avenue South
New York, New York 10016

Please send me the M R books I have checked above. I am
enclosing $_____Check or money order, (no currency or
C.O.D.'s). Enclose price listed for each title plus 35¢ per copy
ordered to cover cost of postage and handling.

Name_____

Address_____

City _____ State_____ Zip_____

MacFadden Romances

#11		44000	**MOONLIGHT INTERLUDE** Sandra Phillipson **ISLAND OF DREAMS** Lucy Merwin $1.95
#12		44011	**A TOUCH OF VELVET** Karen Whitworth **THE SATIN PROMISE** Karen Whitworth $1.95
#15		33014	**HOME FOR SUMMER** Susan Cook $1.25
#16		33015	**CONTINENTAL DREAMS** Patricia Ann Noyes $1.25
#17		33016	**ENCHANTED TWILIGHT** Sandra Phillipson $1.25
#18		33003	**THE STRANGER AND THE SEA** Grace Caldwell $1.25
#19		33018	**FIESTA LA MASQUERADE** Madeleine Brooks $1.25
#20		33019	**BROKEN PRIDE** Elizabeth Gage $1.25

☐ Send me a free list of all your books in print.

MacFadden Romances—
A Division of Kim Publishing Corp.
432 Park Avenue South
New York, New York 10016

Please send me the MR books I have checked above. I am enclosing $_____Check or money order, (no currency or C.O.D.'s). Enclose price listed for each title plus 35¢ per copy ordered to cover cost of postage and handling.

Name_____

Address_____

City _____ State_____ Zip_____

MacFadden Romances

#21		33004	**LOVE MATCH** Hope Richardson	$1.25
#24		44022	**MIDNIGHT JEWEL** Anne Spencer **THE DREAM AND THE DANCE** Laura Daniels	$1.95
#26		33063	**DARE TO LOVE** Violet Fletcher	$1.25
#27		33001	**THE STORM AFFAIR** Dorothy Lippencott	$1.25
#28		33002	**LOVEWINDS** Alicia Adams	$1.25
#29		33028	**SILVER LINING** Elaine Forbes	$1.25
#31		33030	**GOLDEN DREAMS** Elaine Forbes	$1.25
#32		33031	**IF THIS BE LOVE** Leslie Sands	$1.25
#34		33033	**PROMISE OF SPRING** Elaine Forbes	$1.25

☐ Send me a free list of all your books in print.

MacFadden Romances—
A Division of Kim Publishing Corp.
432 Park Avenue South
New York, New York 10016

Please send me the MR books I have checked above. I am
enclosing $_____Check or money order, (no currency or
C.O.D.'s). Enclose price listed for each title plus 35¢ per copy
ordered to cover cost of postage and handling.

Name_____

Address_____

City _____ State_____ Zip_____

MacFadden Romances

#35		44034	**YESTERDAY'S PROMISE** Christina Harding **FLIGHT OF THE FURY** Christina Harding $1.95
#36		44035	**WINTER WHITE** Allison Taylor **TWILIGHT INTERLUDE** Olivia Graham $1.95
#37		33064	**SAFFRON MOON** Lillian Crawford $1.25
#38		33037	**INDIGO ENCOUNTER** Justine Duval $1.25
#39		33038	**THE WINE OF LOVE** Vanessa Cartwright $1.25
#40		33039	**IVORY SANDS** Claudia DuBois $1.25
#41		33041	**CALL OF THE JAGUAR** Elaine Forbes $1.25
#42		33065	**WINTER WISH** Louise Grandville $1.25
#43		33069	**VOICE OF THE JUNGLE** Elaine Forbes $1.25

☐ Send me a free list of all your books in print.

MacFadden Romances—
A Division of Kim Publishing Corp.
432 Park Avenue South
New York, New York 10016

Please send me the MR books I have checked above. I am
enclosing $_____Check or money order, (no currency or
C.O.D.'s). Enclose price listed for each title plus 35¢ per copy
ordered to cover cost of postage and handling.

Name_____

Address_____

City _____ State_____ Zip_____

MacFadden Romances

#65		33078	**DEAR STRANGER** Hope Richardson	$1.25
#66		33079	**MOONLIT SANDS** Alicia Adams	$1.25
#67		33080	**THE SHADOW OF LOVE** Alice Livingston	$1.25
#68		33052	**PRELUDE TO LOVE** Brooke Carpenter	$1.25
#69		33081	**STARLIGHT** **RENDEZVOUS** Dale Bartholomew	$1.25
#70		33082	**LIES OF LOVE** Gail Palmer	$1.25
#71		33083	**LEGACY OF LOVE** Sally Ann Taylor	$1.25
#72		33084	**THE OTHER SIDE** **OF LOVE** Coleen McDonald	$1.25
#73		33085	**INHERIT THE DREAM** Margary Beauchamp	$1.25

☐ Send me a free list of all your books in print.

MacFadden Romances—
A Division of Kim Publishing Corp.
432 Park Avenue South
New York, New York 10016

Please send me the MR books I have checked above. I am
enclosing $_____Check or money order, (no currency or
C.O.D.'s). Enclose price listed for each title plus 35¢ per copy
ordered to cover cost of postage and handling.

Name_____

Address_____

City _____ State_____ Zip_____

MacFadden Romances

#74		33086	**TIME OF TENDERNESS** Alice Livingston	$1.25
#75		33087	**HIGH TIDE OF LOVE** Helen Rollins	$1.25
#76		33088	**SWEET INNOCENT** Alicia Adams	$1.25
#77		33090	**THE GARDEN OF LIGHT** Margary Beauchamp	$1.25
#78		33089	**THE GAELIC HEIRS** Rose Butler	$1.25
#79		33068	**DANGEROUS ROMANCE** Lucy Merwin	$1.25
#80		33101	**FOLLOW THE SUN** Christina Harding	$1.25
#81		33025	**LOVE IN BLOOM** Tracy Baer	1.25
#82		33042	**APPOINTMENT IN ANTIBES** Vanessa Cartwright	$1.25
#83		33099	**THIS LOVE TO SHARE** Marie Porterfield	$1.25

☐ Send me a free list of all your books in print.

MacFadden Romances
A Division of Kim Publishing Corp.
432 Park Avenue South
New York, New York 10016

Please send me the MR books I have checked above. I am
enclosing $_____ Check or money order, (no currency or
C.O.D.'s). Enclose price listed for each title plus 35¢ per copy
ordered to cover cost of postage and handling.

Name_____ _____

Address_____

City _____ State_____ Zip_____